I0654070

# Edge of Chaos

# Edge of Chaos

Book 2

A Tommy Dapino Thriller

TED
GALDI

© 2021 Ted Galdi

All rights reserved. No part of this book may be
reproduced in any form or by any means, electronic or
mechanical, including photocopying, recording, or by
any information storage and retrieval system, without
permission in writing from the publisher.

ISBN: 978-1-7366716-3-4

# ONE

Tommy Dapino isn't used to this. The first black-tie gala in his thirty-two years, a fundraiser for endangered sea animals in La Jolla, California.

His girlfriend Jordana, sitting next to him at a table near the stage, whispers in his ear, "You look so hot in your tux, you might have to meet me in the bathroom before this thing is over."

He hasn't worn a tux since prom. Back in the blue collar neighborhood where he grew up in Queens, New York. Unsure how to tie a bowtie, he picked up a pre-knotted clip-on at the rental place for tonight.

"You don't look too bad in that red dress either," he whispers to Jordana, just above the sound of orchestra music from the eight-piece band. "Instead of walking all the way over to the bathroom, why don't we just go under the table?" He lifts its long white cloth, peeks beneath. "Yeah, that should do."

She slaps his shoulder. "Seriously though, thanks for coming tonight. Sometimes these events are a bit stiff. But my mom knows the organizer, wanted to make sure our family contributed. Hope you're having a good time."

"Definitely an experience. Speaking of a good time, I'm going to grab another Jack. Want anything?"

She flashes him a thumbs-up, returns to her arugula salad.

He ventures to the bar through twosomes and threesomes engaged in conversation. And says to the server, "Hey bud. Let's do another for me. And a Goose and cranberry for my girl."

The bartender starts on the drinks. Tommy tips him, setting a five on the countertop. Then turns to a projector behind the band cycling through still photos of sea animals with big, needy eyes.

He hears a snicker from the seventyish man beside him. His gaze on Tommy's wrist.

"Can I help you with something?" Tommy asks.

"No thank you, young man. I don't need any help."

"Well, is something funny then? I like jokes. Did I miss one?"

The man holds a champagne glass, a drunk glaze to his eyes. "Something may be funny to me. But I doubt it would be to you."

Tommy folds his hands, grins. "My sense of humor casts a wide net."

"Your watch. It's . . . well . . . fake." Another snicker.

Tommy glances at his Patek Philippe, a family heirloom from his deceased grandfather, the only item of value passed down the Dapino lineage. Afraid of scratching it, Tommy only wears it on the specialist of occasions.

"It's not fake," he says.

"I own seventeen jewelry stores across Southern California. Been in the business my whole life. Spotting phonies is my livelihood. And that, fine fellow, is a phony." The man turns to his date, a much younger woman with a pompous haircut drinking a martini. They both giggle.

Tommy grabs the glass of Jack waiting on the bar, swigs it, says to him, "I can spot phonies too. With all those jewelry stores you own, I'm surprised you couldn't afford a better toupee. Where did you buy that thing, Party City?"

The man's date gasps, throws her martini in Tommy's face.

"Christ," Tommy says.

The bartender glimpses him. "You spill?"

"You didn't see that?" Tommy yells. Heads turn to him.

"See what?"

"I didn't spill anything. She . . . you didn't see what she just did?"

The bartender shrugs.

Jordana trots over, her long black ponytail bobbing. "Did I just hear you yell? What's going on?"

"Nothing," Tommy says, liquid dripping off his cheeks.

"That acquaintance of yours is rude, is what's going on," the martini-chucking lady says, nose angled up.

"You insulted this woman?" Jordana asks.

"What? No. You're blaming this on me?"

A mid-twenties man in an ascot walks up, eyeballs angry-looking Tommy. "Everything all right, Jordana?"

"Who the hell is this asshole?" Tommy asks.

"Whoa," Jordana says. "A family friend from Napa. Chill out." She glimpses the inquisitive faces around them, her cheeks reddening. Then glances at the exit.

"If your date from Queens is embarrassing you around your Napa friends," Tommy says, "why don't you just leave?" He points the way she's looking.

"I think I do need some air. Dry yourself off. I'll . . . be back." She cuts between the dozen or so onlookers, leaves the event hall.

Tommy lets out a long breath, dips his gaze to the floor. He walks to the bathroom. Cleans himself up. And lingers inside a stall, avoiding the judgmental stares of all those rich people. He inspects the details of his watch, catches a couple imperfections.

In about fifteen minutes, he drums up the nerve to wander back into the ballroom, the band playing a swing song. No Jordana by the bar. No Jordana at their table. She must still be outside.

That bullshit before was not his fault, but he'll try to make it right. Not worth a fight. He steps out of the Vista Banquet building into the San Diego May weather, a low-seventies breeze, a subtle sway to the palm trees.

No Jordana on the deck. He peers at the cove across the street. No Jordana on the beach, just the sprawling black of nighttime sand and sea. He observes the line of storefronts about a quarter mile away, just a couple still lit at this hour.

Maybe she's getting a coffee at the Starbucks. He treads a windy pathway, the music from the gala softening behind him. Soon he can just hear the crash of ocean against cliffs.

A familiar glimmer of light on the ground in an alley. A buckle on Jordana's clutch purse. He dashes to it, picks it up. A few splotches on the pink leather.

Blood.

His heart bangs. He opens the purse, her phone still inside, no way to reach her. He scrolls through it for an indication of what may've happened. No recent calls or texts.

"Hands up," a voice hollers.

Tommy looks toward it. Two policemen point guns at him.

# TWO

Tommy's lean-muscled, six-one body slumps over a metal stool in a windowless, eight-by-ten police interrogation room, an overhead lamp casting a dim light on the chipped, gray walls. A rattle from some unseen plumbing.

The door opens. A fortyish redheaded man enters, a detective badge at his waist. He sits at the same side of the table as Tommy, stares him down for a couple seconds, and says, "According to statistics, when a woman goes missing, the boyfriend or husband is often to blame."

"According to statistics, when a man has adult acne, lack of hygiene versus hormones is often to blame."

A reflexive raise of the detective's hand over a zit on his chin. He opens a manila folder, inside files with

Tommy's name. "I see you did two years in the Attica Correctional Facility in New York."

"For a crime I didn't commit."

"So the cops in New York wrongfully accused you then? And you believe the ones in California did again tonight?"

"Bad luck I guess."

"Hope you don't develop a dice habit when you go back to prison. You might lose all your cigarettes."

"You don't have enough to charge me with shit. I know how this works. I'm in the industry."

The detective chuckles. "File says you work for some PI agency I never heard of. Canven Investigative Solutions? What's your day-to-day like? Following around insurance cheats, waiting for them to take off their neck braces for a photo op? Or maybe you don't even deal with human beings. Missing pets, is that it? You track down loose cats? Got yourself a toolbelt equipped with squeaky toys?"

A slow exhale from Tommy. "So you like statistics. We PIs know this one . . . when people go missing, with each passing hour, the chances of finding them plummet, almost hitting zero at seventy-two hours. If you think I'm behind Jordana's disappearance, you're clearly too incompetent to find her before then. Now let me out of here so I can."

"Jordana. Yes, the lovely Jordana. Unlike you, she is actually in the industry. If I were her, I'd just live on a yacht spending daddy's wine fortune. But she decided to get a job with the Federal Bureau of Investigation." He whistles. "Commendable. But doesn't bode well for you. Not only is my team searching for her. The feds too. And I'm sure her family already has a well-paid PI on retainer. One from a firm with a slightly better reputation than Canven. When she's found, and gives her testimony, the trouble you're in will only get worse."

"What trouble? I still don't even know what crime I'm being accused of."

"Here's how I see it. Any minute now, your masked buddy in the gray van is—"

"A masked buddy? What gray van?"

"He is going to call up Jordana's father. And ask him to send a couple million dollars of cryptocurrency to an untraceable account to get his daughter back."

"I didn't know a single person at that fundraiser besides her. No buddy of mine was there."

"Our witness saw another man. Tall, fit, ski mask."

"What witness?"

"Name is confidential."

"How am I supposed to defend myself against an accusation if you won't even give me the details of it?"

"I can give you this . . . we looked at security-camera footage at the banquet hall. Jordana walked out at fourteen minutes past eight. The nine-one-one call from the witness came in nineteen minutes and fifty-six seconds after. You walked out right after she was forced into the van."

Tommy shakes his head. "So my masked friend kidnaps Jordana. Then I decide to stroll to the crime scene immediately after. Why the hell would I do that?"

"Guessing he called you on a burner, said she dropped her purse during their scuffle. You were just cleaning up the loose end."

"I have a key to her apartment. If I was going to have someone kidnap her, why not send him there in the middle of the night? Why do it at a crowded ball?"

"A high-rise apartment building like hers is way riskier. People all over. The ball was only crowded inside. Which is why you made a scene, provoked her to go outside to the quiet street."

"I didn't make any scene," he shouts. "Some woman threw a drink in my face. She made the scene."

"On surveillance, we did notice the woman throwing the drink in your face. A guy on my team interviewed her. She said she did it only after you insulted her date."

"He insulted me first."

"Not a single guest we spoke to said they overheard that. You've got a smart mouth, Dapino. I think you were going around that ball looking to piss someone off. Looking to cause a commotion, start a fight with Jordana over it, then tell her to cool off outside. The tape shows you talking to her, pointing at the door. Your friend was waiting out there to snatch her. You'd split the ransom. And when she was let go, pretend you were oblivious. Am I close?"

"You're about as close as your wife is when she tells you she's having an orgasm."

The detective stands, clasps Tommy's tuxedo shirt. "Watch it, you fucking wop." His bad breath wafts into Tommy's nose. "Looks like you're going to be charged with suspicion of kidnapping. Typically an initial bail of a hundred thousand dollars."

"I don't have the cash to put up for that."

The detective smirks. "More bad luck."

# THREE

Tommy paces a block of a Downtown jail among a hundred fifty or so just-arrested men. A clamor of voices, slamming gates, buzzers. His watch is off, confiscated with his phone, wallet, and keys. He is the only person in a tuxedo.

Getting his ass out of here is a must. His eyes flick to a barred window. Outside it a tower topped with two ugly guards clutching rifles. Plenty more armed enforcers inside. Getting past them all seems impossible.

"Yo homes," a prisoner says.

Tommy turns to a short but muscular Latino, a Grim Reaper tattoo on his forearm, and says, "Yeah?"

"It's true what I hear walking around in here?"

"I wasn't walking around with you, was I? How should I know?"

The Latino rubs his nose. "You were railing some hot FBI agent, then you iced the bitch. I always wanted to fuck a fed. And kill one. Doing both . . . well . . . a man could only dream. It'd be a pleasure to shake your hand."

Tommy chuckles. "If you call my girlfriend a bitch again, you won't be able to walk around here anymore. Just roll."

The prisoner holds a stare on Tommy. "Oh, it's like that, White boy?"

Two other inked-up Latinos mosey over, glare at Tommy.

"Once you put me in a wheelchair," the one with the Reaper tat says, "at least I'll have some friends to push me around."

Tommy peers at the two friends. "I'd rethink that. The first is cross-eyed and the second has BO. If one pushed you, you'd probably bang into walls." He sniffs the second, winces. "And if this guy did, you might vomit into your lap."

Fists clenching, the Latinos circle the White guy in the tux. About fifteen prisoners huddle around as if ready for a show. "Fuck this pussy up," one shouts.

Another flips off Tommy. "You gonna get it, son. Oh you gonna eat it."

The Latinos blurt some Spanish, then charge at Tommy among cries of bloodlust from the spectators.

Tommy kicks the tallest one on in the gut. He hunches forward. Tommy knees him in the bridge of the nose, his head snapping back, blood sprinkling.

An arm wraps Tommy's throat, a chokehold from behind. He dips his skull a few inches forward, then springs it backward, thwacking the choker's chin. Tommy spins out of his grasp, jabs him in the throat, then elbows his temple. He crumples to the floor.

The third attacker hurls a right hook at Tommy's head. It catches his jaw, pain rumbling up to his cheekbone. The Latino throws a body blow. Tommy sidesteps it, grabs the guy's wrist, and elbows the center of his arm, snapping his humerus. He howls.

"Out of my way dickheads," an incoming guard shouts, shoving observers.

Tommy gazes down at his three bested challengers, a splatter of blood on the floor between them. Among them is his facedown clip-on bowtie, must've fallen off during the brawl.

He has an idea.

He slips the bowtie into his pocket. Then the guard tackles him to the floor.

# FOUR

Seventeen hours since Jordana's disappearance.

The redheaded detective on her case, Finch, yanks open the sock drawer in Tommy's bedroom. He squints in the San Diego sun shooting through the window, a dry plant on the sill.

He scours the drawer. "Nothing useful in here either. How we looking out there?"

A police computer-forensics technician on Tommy's laptop says, "Gmail. Purchases on Amazon. Seems like he's learning how to cook, a bunch of YouTube videos on it. Nothing so far indicative of a ransom scheme."

"Well . . . keep looking."

A knock on the ajar front door of Tommy's house, a small, one-story surf shack built in the 1970s.

"This is an investigation scene," Finch says. "We

have a court order. Please go away."

"I know the man who lives here," a female voice says from the stoop.

"That's of no concern to me."

"It should be." A woman in her late forties pushes open the door. She's about two hundred pounds, most of them muscle.

"Are you trying to get arrested, lady?"

"I'm not much of a lady. And I don't think you have the authority to arrest me." She reveals a badge. "Helga Wichita. Special Agent in Charge. FBI San Diego."

He swallows. "I've . . . yes. Our office has worked closely with yours on . . . countless . . . I've seen your name on reports, just never knew what you looked like, ma'am. Sorry."

She marches inside. A pile of toiletries on the floor, open cabinets, clothing strewn about the couch and bed. Her attention drifts to a trio of framed photographs on the wall of Tommy and Jordana at a concert with beers, on Jet Skis making funny faces, dressed up for Halloween as John Travolta and Uma Thurman's characters in *Pulp Fiction*.

"Already a day since she went missing," Wichita says. "Statistically, every hour after—"

"With all due respect, I know the data."

"With all due respect, do you know anything else about missing-persons cases?"

"Excuse me?"

"You've got the wrong guy."

A moment. "Once we get Dapino's phone records, we're confident we can narrow down who his accomplice was. Then all we need to—"

"Dapino didn't have an accomplice."

"The eyewitness was certain. She said—"

"I'm not arguing the witness spotted someone. But where's the evidence that someone was working with Dapino?"

"Dapino was standing at the scene of the crime holding an object of hers with blood on it. And when a billionaire heiress goes missing, odds are ransom is the motive. He's a two-bit PI who probably has a couple thousand bucks in his name."

She chuckles. "Who told you he was two-bit?"

"I checked out that company he works for. Canven. Found nothing about them."

"That's by design. Canven doesn't take on cases from the general public. They only work on sensitive, high-profile ones. Secrecy is paramount."

Finch looks away, at a pair of Tommy's dumbbells on the floor. "How did a guy like Dapino, with no college or formal investigative training, end up there?"

"I made a personal referral after he helped us out on a probe last year. He has an X factor the more polished investigators lack. Which makes him perfectly suited for jobs that require a certain . . . grit."

Finch chuckles. "You mean an ex-con factor?"

"Laugh all you want. His stint in Attica was actually a benefit for this line of work. He went into that hell hole with no gang affiliation. In a situation like that, you're forced to develop survival skills quickly. How to read people, detect a threat from the slightest gesture. How to deceive to avoid a fight. And if a fight is unavoidable . . . how to kick the shit out of your opponent and win."

"You know what else you learn in a place like Attica? How to be a better criminal. You're surrounded by cons. You talk. You learn what worked for them on the outside. Maybe that's where he heard about the lucrative art of high-net-worth kidnapping."

"Apparently he didn't even ask about salary in his Canven interview. Money isn't a major motivator for him. He wouldn't go through all this for a few bucks."

Finch folds his arms. "Money possibly wasn't a motivator for him in the past. Which is why he doesn't have much. Started hooking up with a rich girl. Saw the way she lived. Began resenting her for being born into it. Motivations changed."

"Not to this degree. Kidnapping your own girl-friend?"

"A relationship with someone from a higher social class can screw with your head. Bring out insecurities you never knew were there. Push you to extremes to compensate. A number of marriages start off great, then end in murder. The most common reason a spouse kills another is jealousy. The second most, financial gain. Dapino was jealous of her money, and had plenty to gain asking for some."

"I've been in communication with Jordana's parents. They stayed up all night. No ransom demands came in."

"Maybe Dapino's partner is spooked because of the arrest. Could've called the whole thing off. Still doesn't change the fact they abducted her. Still doesn't change the fact Dapino should be locked up."

"Jordana's parents certainly don't think he should. They told me he spent a long weekend with the family up in Napa. They got to know him, like him, doubt he'd ever hurt Jordana."

"Did you just come here to shit on my investigation? Or does the FBI have a better theory than ours?"

"We certainly do."

"So you identified a different suspect?"

A moment. "Not yet. But we will."

"Well, I'd love to hear this theory. But unless it

leads to an arrest, of a suspect that's a better fit for this than mine, Dapino stays behind bars."

# FIVE

In an orange jumpsuit, Tommy sits behind plexiglass in the jailhouse. Hair messy, eyes bloodshot. A Black prisoner to his left grips a cord phone with one hand, his other pressed to the glass. A woman on the opposite side holds her palm to his.

"They did me wrong, baby," he says. "My lawyer, he up on it. Going to get me out. Then I'm going to kiss that fine ass up and down. You know how much I love you?"

To Tommy's right, a few seats down, a Latino prisoner with a tear-drop face tat scowls at him.

The three guys he pulverized last night seem to have quite a few pals in here. The longer he's locked up, the higher the odds one will shove a shiv into his back.

Tommy looks ahead. Through the plexiglass he

spots his best friend, Josh Hess. Same age, endearing face, five foot six. He moved to San Diego from New York a few months ago to be close to Tommy. Josh sits on a stool and picks up a phone.

"T, I'm shaking," he says.

"Don't shake. We need—"

"Jordana just gone. How—"

"I know. I know."

"I had a bad feeling about that rich-person party you went to. Queens guys like us don't belong at things like that. A ballroom? An orchestra? No way that was ending well for you, T."

"The party's over. I need to focus on the future. The immediate future. If I don't, Jordana's going to end up dead."

"When I match with a girl on a dating app, I sometimes send Jordana a screenshot of the profile and she gives me advice on an opening line. As busy as she is with that FBI job, she gets back to me within ten minutes. Who would want someone like that dead? Huh?"

"I'm going to find out. And make the prick pay."

"Difficult to do in here, no?"

"Very difficult to do in here."

"You got the other guys from your PI agency on this?"

"I tried. My boss nicely told me the firm had no choice but to disassociate itself from me after my arrest. I told him I'll be disassociating myself from them too. And wasn't as nice."

"Oh jeez. And you obviously can't go to the cops for help."

"I realize, Josh. Thank you."

"Then who you going to rely on?"

A moment. "You."

A befuddled look on Josh. "Me?"

"Just in the beginning. I'll take it from there."

"The beginning of what?"

Tommy inches up to the glass. Presses his palm against it. Scribbled on it in pen is *ESCAPE*.

"No," Josh says. "Oh no. No, no. no."

"I only trust two people in San Diego. The first is Jordana. And the second is you."

Josh throws an anxious look over his right shoulder, then left, and whispers, "The cable guy accidentally gave me HBO sophomore year of college. And I reported the error in fear of being exposed as a criminal."

"I'll do all the heavy lifting. I just need you to handle a few basic moves."

"I'll hack the moves up. Then wind up on the other side of the glass with you."

Tommy rubs his forehead. "Remember rec baseball in sixth grade, second round of the playoffs when we were down one in the bottom of the last inning?"

"Of course I remember."

"Brad Mahoney on the hill, who threw like eighty as a twelve-year-old. You step up to the plate with two outs. Everyone in the stands was expecting him to whiff you in three pitches. To be honest, I was too. But what happened instead? You knocked a Goddamn rope into the left-center gap, drove in two to win."

"Mahoney kicking that cooler. I'll never forget it."

"You came up clutch then. And I know you can now."

Josh is quiet for a while. A deep breath. "What the hell do you need from me?"

Tommy eyeballs the guard by the wall. Waits for his gaze to move off him. Then unzips the top of his jumpsuit, revealing pen-written instructions on his chest.

# SIX

Thirty-nine hours since Jordana's disappearance.

A silver-and-green bus with *California Correc-tions & Rehabilitation Department* on the side moves through Downtown San Diego around lunchtime on Monday, the streets bustling with office workers on break.

Tommy rides on the transport vehicle in his orange jumpsuit, a metal bracelet around each ankle, connected with a short chain restricting his legs' range of motion. A second chain around his waist. A third extends from it to his handcuffs, preventing his arms from moving more than a few inches.

Seven other shackled men sit among him on the four-minute drive from jail to a courthouse for arraignments. A prisoner hums a song.

"Shut up," a tall, square-jawed guard yells.

He watches the prisoners while the second guard monitors busy Broadway out the window. The first's gaze locks with Tommy's. The guard keeps it on him for two seconds, then moves it to the inmate behind. Two seconds on him. The guard's attention switches to a prisoner across the aisle.

Tommy slides his tongue between his teeth and right cheek. And feels around for metal. He dips his head and frees into his lap an inch-long, nickel-plated object. His bowtie clip.

When he was arrested, and his belongings con-fiscated, the cops must've assumed he was wearing a traditional bowtie, the norm at high-end fundraisers, not one with a metal clip. He hid it under the pillow in his cell and spent a couple hours last night whittling it down against the sharp edge of his bedframe.

He maneuvers the thinned tip of the clip into the keyhole of his left handcuff. Poking. Twisting. More poking. Adjusting. A bit of twisting, more adjusting. Another poke. Another twist.

A soft click inside the casing.

He coughs on purpose while nudging the brace-let's ratchet teeth outward. Coughs again, nudges again, the shackle still on, yet wide enough to slip a hand through.

The courthouse emerges out the window. No more than twenty seconds till they arrive. He starts on his right bracelet. Twisting and poking until he hears a soft click. A couple more coughs to mask the loosening sound.

"You have emphysema or something, Dapino?" the tall guard shouts.

"No sir. Just a sore throat. Sorry."

"Cough into your shoulder next time. If you get me sick, I swear to Christ, I'll shove my nightstick so far up your ass it'll count as a daily meal."

"Understood, sir."

The bus coasts to a stop at a courthouse side door. Tommy takes a deep breath, wondering if Josh came through for him.

"Stand up, walk out one by one starting at the front," the shorter guard says. He steps outside, his partner observing the inmates from inside.

The first prisoner stands and takes restricted, awkward steps down the stairs and out the door. Four other men file out behind him. Tommy rises, keeping his hands close to his body, concealing the slack in his bracelets.

He moves ahead. The cheap rubber sandals they issued him reach the sidewalk. He glances left. High-rise buildings, streetlamps. He glances right. A jolt of excitement in his stomach. As intended, Josh's motorized scooter is parked on the sidewalk about ten feet away.

The last of the inmates debusses. A court bailiff opens the building door. Arms folded, Detective Finch leans against a hallway wall. He smirks when his eyes meet Tommy's.

The prisoners file through the doorway. Just before Tommy does, he looks back at the street and screams, "Holy shit, that guy has a bomb."

All heads snap that direction. Tommy takes off running in a short-step motion. The tall guard notices and lunges toward him. Tommy slips his hands out of his bracelets, cocks his right back, and slugs him in the mouth. He topples onto his back, a tooth spinning on the sidewalk beside him.

His partner holds back the cheering inmates while Detective Finch flies out of the doorway. Tommy shuffles toward the scooter. Finch sprints up to him, says,

"Get back here you son of a bitch."

Tommy grabs the scooter's handlebars and swings the platform at Finch, nailing his ankle, taking his legs out. He goes airborne for a moment, then crashes down, his head thumping the pavement. Tommy jumps on the scooter and twists the key Josh left in the ignition.

He squeezes the throttle. The scooter zooms ahead, behind him the sound of the inmates whistling and the guards stammering into their radios.

Tommy turns left. Pedestrians gawk at the chain-wrapped young man in the orange jumpsuit zipping by at forty miles per hour.

He advances another two blocks. The sound of police sirens in the distance. He takes a second left onto Birch Avenue. Josh's parked white Nissan Sentra comes into view.

The scooter screeches to a stop behind it. "Here," Tommy says.

Josh notices him in the rearview mirror, starts the engine, and pops the hatch. Tommy chucks the scooter into the trunk and dives in. He slams it shut. Josh drives away.

# SEVEN

Josh's trunk must be a hundred degrees. Tommy feels around the darkness, his hand meeting the burner phone waiting for him. He presses the keypad, a glimmer from the screen providing some visibility. With the bowtie clip, he picks the padlock on his waist chain, then contorts his body in the tight space to reach his ankles, undoes their shackles, then contorts his body again to slip out of the jail uniform.

He changes into clothes waiting for him in a shopping bag. Jeans, sneakers, and a yellow tee shirt with a tiger on it. His neck cramps from all the twisting and turning.

He calls Josh.

"Holy shit," Josh says. "Did we just pull that off?"

"We didn't pull anything off. Not yet at least. You hear those sirens? We got to get to the campground before they find us." A moment. "What's with the tiger shirt by the way? I look like I'm about to deal Molly behind a Porta-Potty at an EDM festival."

"I figured if I was grabbing you fresh threads, I might as well throw in a dash of style."

"Jesus. Just ... keep your eyes on the road. Do not get pulled over."

"T, I'm at ten and two. Three MPH under the limit. Rocking the Bluetooth."

"Good. Hey man, I owe you for this."

"You don't owe me anything. You're my best friend. And if Jordana is in danger, how could I not help?"

"Glad you like her that much. She likes you too."

"I've gotten along with all your girls over the years. Makes it hard when you eventually break up with them."

"Who said I was planning on breaking up with Jordana?"

"No one. Just ... for whatever reason, none of your relationships seem to last." A pause. "Forget I said it."

Tommy, good at impressions, says in Josh's voice, "Hi, I'm Josh. I've spent more romantic nights with Jergens bottles than girls, but I somehow feel entitled to judge all Tommy's relationships."

Silence on the other line for a while.

"Eh," Tommy says in his own voice. "That was ... I was out of line. Sorry."

"It isn't even true. I didn't want to jinx it so didn't say anything, but I met a girl named Michelle at Starbucks last week. And we went on a date. Taco Tuesday. And it went really well. And I like her a lot. And I think she likes me too. Maybe also a lot. So ... yeah."

"Happy for you."

A moment. "Uh oh."

"What oh?"

"Police checkpoint. Are they looking for you? Jeez. Is this for us? I'll go another way."

"If one road is blocked by now, others likely are too. They're trying to pen me in."

"T, I'm starting to shake. I'm—"

"Don't shake. If the cops see you bugging out through the windshield they're going to know something's up."

"Something is up. I have an escaped felon in my trunk. They could make me open it."

"Look, this was all my idea. I'm not letting you get pinched for aiding and abetting. I can't be near you right now."

"How're we going to do that?"

Tommy's mind races through possible solutions. "Turn onto a side street. Stop when you see a manhole."

# EIGHT

Bright sunlight pours into Josh's trunk as the hatch lifts, stinging Tommy's darkness-adjusted eyes. He steps out with the tire iron from the car's spare-attachment toolkit.

"What're you planning on doing with that?" Josh asks.

"Better you don't know. Plausible deniability. Where's the police checkpoint?"

Josh points north. "About a thousand feet that way."

"If the cops notice you with me back here, you're going down too. Drive away."

"Are you planning on smashing them over the head with that tool thing?"

"Get out of here, Josh, or I'm going to smash you over the head with it."

"Yikes. All right."

"Stay in the general area. And keep your eyes on your phone. I'm going to need you again in a bit."

"To do—"

"Just go."

Josh scampers back to the driver's seat and motors away.

Tommy's gaze shifts to the manhole cover on the street. In his periphery, he notices the back of a bakery. A lady in a chef's hat peers at him through a window as police sirens blare. She glimpses the tire iron in his hand, her expression troubled. Then she disappears from sight.

"Shit," Tommy mutters. He shimmies an end of the tire iron through a tiny hole in the sewer cover and pushes down on the other, applying it as a lever. He grunts. The lid must weigh two hundred pounds. It rises an inch. Another grunt. Another inch. Tommy kicks it to the side, revealing an underground chute.

He descends its ladder rungs. The stench of the city's underbelly burrows into his nostrils. He hops down to the surface. A small splash, the chill of liquid filth on his ankles.

He turns on his new phone's flashlight. The beam thrashes in front of him as he sprints through the tunnel. Based on the checkpoint location, the cops believe Tommy's no more than a thousand feet from here. He needs to run beyond that distance before they widen the search radius.

Advancing northward on a winding path, he inhales mouthfuls of reeking air. About ten minutes pass. The roar of traffic overhead. He stops under another sewer lid, climbs a ladder up to it. He watches the bits of daylight through the lid's holes. They go dark when a car zooms past.

He counts *Mississippis* in his head. At *seven* the daylight darkens again. He observes the lid for another minute and averages about six seconds between cars at the current rhythm of traffic.

The daylight fades again. He punches the lid with the tire iron and pushes upward. Specks of dirt scrape off the metal into his right eye.

"Goddammit," he says, his vision blurry. Without both eyes functional, his depth perception will be skewed, which could prove fatal. He rubs the itchy eye. Blinks. Rubs again. Blinks again. The blur a bit better.

With his hands, he muscles the sewer cover to the side. The wheels of a honking car swerve around him.

He pops his head aboveground. A road with two lanes, his face in the middle of one. An SUV barrels toward him. He leaps outside, his palms and chest scraping the asphalt. The SUV's horn hollers at him. He rolls out of the collision path.

A couple deep breaths. He scrambles to his feet, then to the sidewalk, and calls Josh.

"Yo," Josh says. "How you—"

"Clarington Medical Partners."

"Huh?"

"It's some business I'm by. Beyond the checkpoint. Google Maps it. Get your ass over here. I'll be in the alley."

"Got it. Clarence Medical—"

"Clarington. Also, we won't be able to make it all the way out to the campground anymore."

"What? Why?"

"Some pastry-chef lady. She was giving me a dirty look when you dropped me off. Guessing she saw me get out of your trunk. She could've connected me to the sirens, hit up the cops with your car's make and model. They could already have an APB out for it."

"Son of a bitch."

"We've got to get your whip off the road as soon as you pick me up. Duck out indoors, someplace close, plan the next move."

"Indoors where?"

Tommy is quiet for a couple seconds.

"Oh no T, not there," Josh says. "That's worse than the car. At least the car has a trunk to hide you in."

"I . . . yeah, I realize. I will do everything in my power to make sure nobody finds me there."

A pause. "I changed my mind. You do owe me for this. A trip. Someplace expensive."

# NINE

Head low, Tommy strides toward the door of Josh's apartment, a third-story unit in an older Downtown building. Tommy holds Josh's laptop, taken from his car, now out of public view in the garage.

Josh twists the knob and they enter a one-bedroom apartment decorated with movie posters.

Tommy notices a new addition to the home. "Whoa, whoa, whoa. What the hell is that?"

"Just got it installed. It's a beaut, huh T?"

Tommy gazes at a fish tank with half a dozen live lobsters inside. "Come on, man."

"I figured since I live by the beach now, I should incorporate an aquatic motif into my personal space. And traditional fish tanks are just ... cliche. Lobster tanks are always a great feature in seafood-restaurant lobbies. Why not bring that type of elegant allure into the home?"

Tommy is silent for a few seconds. "Are you going to eat them?"

"I love shellfish. But no, not these. If I pound them, I'll just have a big glass box of water in my living room. And who needs that?"

"So they're what, then? Like your pets?"

"You're looking too deeply into this. It's a pure ambience play."

"Oh, it definitely creates an ambience." Tommy sits at Josh's desk, opens the laptop, and does a Google search for "Vista Banquet," the event hall that hosted the gala he and Jordana attended.

He clicks into the map's street view, navigates to where the cops arrested him, and conducts a three-sixty sweep, noting four establishments with a view into the alley.

"Check this out," he says. "An art gallery. A bank. A dentist. What do these three businesses have in common?"

Josh stares at the screen. "You turn into the Riddler when you were in jail? I don't know."

"They're the kinds of businesses that close before eight PM. Around when Jordana went missing."

"So?"

Tommy zooms in on the fourth, Gojo Fro-Yo. "Frozen yogurt. These places are usually open till at least ten. And the counter is facing the window."

"So?"

"So I know the eyewitness of Jordana's kidnap."

Josh nods. "Whoever was working the counter at Gojo Fro-Yo two nights ago."

Tommy gives him a thumbs-up, then looks up the shop's phone number, dials it on his burner.

"Gojo," a deadpan male voice says on the other line.

"Good afternoon. I'm with the San Diego Police Department. Calling about a witness interview we conducted the night before last with one of your employees."

"The kidnap thing?"

"Is the witness in?"

"She doesn't work the dayshift."

"Do you have a cell number I can reach her on?"

"You didn't get it the other night?"

"I'm sure a colleague did. But I wasn't on the scene and don't . . . see it written down on the file in front of me."

"I don't know if she's going to want to talk about this again. She's still pretty shook up. Saw some chick get punched out. Blood all over the place."

Anger courses through Tommy imagining the piece of shit in the ski mask laying a hand on his girlfriend. Struggling to keep his voice composed, he says, "I will be . . . mindful of her emotional state."

"Umm, well, we have an employee directory in a drawer in the back. One sec." A cheesy Gojo Fro-Yo jingle plays. The attendant comes back on the line, provides a cell number.

Tommy memorizes it. "Thank you." He hangs up, calls the witness.

"Hello?" a youthful female voice says, Latina accent.

"Hi miss. This is Officer Hartley from the San Diego Police Department. I'm a colleague of Detective Finch."

"Oh. Hey."

"Sorry to be a bother. I realize my department already has a statement from you, but I was hoping you could give me your account directly. I have a few questions, want to go through them chronologically against your timeline. Make sure I don't miss any-thing."

"The internet says one of the guys broke out of jail this morning. That true?"

"I . . . I can't comment on that."

"Well, like, maybe you should. What if I'm in danger and shit?"

"You have no reason to be in danger."

"What if he knows I called the cops on him and his partner man and he comes to like . . . get me? You know . . . revenge."

"I can promise you he won't."

"So he did escape then?"

"Uh. Again, I'm not supposed to comment on that."

"You got questions for me. But I got 'em for you too, papi. Why this gotta be one-way?"

"I can . . . fine. I'll address your questions. But after I ask you mine. So, what first got your attention that night?"

"A scream. I heard a girl scream."

A knock on Josh's apartment door. He and Tom-my's heads whip toward the curtain-covered window.

"Excuse me one second," Tommy says into the phone. He points at the window.

Josh paces to it. Peels back the curtain, then whisks it shut.

"What?" Tommy whispers.

"Two cops," Josh replies in a louder whisper. "How the hell do they already know you're here?"

Tommy thinks. "They don't."

"They're standing at the door, literally—"

"A SWAT team would've kicked it down if they knew I was here. The jail-visitor log from yesterday. They saw your name. Just a routine follow-up. Play it cool and this will go away."

"When have I ever been able to play anything cool?"

# TEN

The cops at the door knock again. In his deep voice, one says, "Mister Hess, this is Officer Washington with the SDPD. We saw the curtain move. We know you're in there. We just need a few minutes of your time."

Josh, pacing, whispers to Tommy, "Can I just ignore them?"

"That'll only make them suspicious. I'm going to bounce until they leave. Keep cool. Make something up. Acting. Like in the movies."

"Acting. Right, acting."

"Yo, everything all right, mister cop?" the frozen-yogurt attendant asks, her voice muffled under Tommy's palm.

"Sorry about that, miss. Something . . . came up. I've got to call you back."

"What about my questions about this escaped-prisoner shit? You promised me you'd—"

He hangs up. Then opens the sliding-glass door at the rear of the apartment, steps onto the balcony. He hops onto its top rail, grips two of its bars, and lowers himself toward the unit beneath Josh's.

The sound of *The Price Is Right* flows through the neighbor's open window. A seventyish woman sits in a rocking chair fixated on her TV. Tommy listens to the gameshow. The crowd is quiet, watching a wheel spin. His elbows tighten supporting his bodyweight.

The wheel stops. The crowd cheers. Tommy drops his feet onto the woman's balcony railing, the metallic rattle damped by the TV noise. He jumps, crashes onto the grass.

A pain in his hip, he rises to his feet, dashes to the bushes, hides behind them. He watches the police cruiser parked in the street in front of the building.

In fifteen minutes or so two cops enter the vehicle and drive away. Josh calls him.

"You had to see me, T," Josh says. "Acted all surprised when they told me you busted out. It was pure Pacino."

"The police shouldn't bother us here again. I'm coming back up."

Tommy hangs up, trots toward the apartment complex. His phone vibrates. A new text message from the frozen-yogurt attendant's number:

*I just called detective finch to ask him about the escaped prisnr. he said ur probably him. Stop contacting me SICKO.*

Tommy rubs his temples. Then kicks a plastic garbage can, a thud echoing.

Josh steps onto his balcony. "You all right down there, chief?"

"No. My pipeline to intel has just been blocked."

"What happened?"

"I'll . . . explain later. I have a backup plan." A moment. "But it's not pretty."

"What is it?"

"Again, later. Toss down a credit card, a hat, and a pair of sunglasses."

"For what?"

"Jesus Josh. Just do it."

Josh nods, disappears inside. In about a minute he surfaces with a plastic bag with the items, drops it to ground level.

Tommy puts on the shades and Yankees cap, pulling it low to obscure his face, then slips the credit card in his pocket, turns off his phone, and chucks it in the trashcan.

"What you do that for?" Josh asks.

"It's been compromised. The police likely have the number and know it's mine, could trace the signal."

"How am I supposed to get in touch with you?"

"You can't. I'll try to reach out. Somehow."

"Oh man. Okay, okay."

"You did good today, Josh."

Josh smiles.

"Love you buddy," Tommy says.

"Love you too. Don't get arrested. Don't die."

Tommy holds up two crossed fingers, then hops a fence. He treads a sidewalk until noticing a taxi. He hails it.

"Where to?" the cabbie asks.

"Sorrento Valley."

"Address?"

"I, uh, don't have an address. Just remember what the house looks like, the area around it."

"Give me a second. Let me find my photo album

with a picture of every house and every tree in Sorrento Valley."

Tommy huffs. "Just drop me off in the middle of town."

He'll have to walk around until recognizing a landmark, hoping the cops don't recognize him first.

# ELEVEN

Forty-four hours since Jordana's disappearance.

Tommy needed over three of them to skulk through Sorrento Valley to find this house, hiding in neighborhood bushes whenever the black and white of a cop car appeared in the distance. Day has turned to early evening, the sky purplish as he waits in a backyard gazebo. Nobody home, no sounds besides the occasional squawk of a bird.

He gazes at the patio's grill, recalling the last time he was here, about a month ago with Jordana for a barbecue. She wore a light-blue dress and drank mimosas. Said she liked an orange slice on the rim of her glass. The party host led them inside. Jordana cut up an orange, gave a wedge to Tommy. He took a bite, more juice than expected, streaks running from his mouth down his chin. She giggled dabbing it with her finger. Called him a citrus vampire. He said that would be a good name for a band.

He thinks about her until the rumble of an engine shakes the quiet. A black Dodge Durango pulling into the driveway. In the driver's seat is the broad, muscled upper body of Helga Wichita, Special Agent in Charge of the FBI's San Diego branch.

She exits with a laptop bag, paces toward the house. Tommy jogs to the yard gate, opens it.

Her head pivots to the noise. Her fists go up. The right one hurtles at his head.

He ducks. "Easy."

She throws a left hook. He evades it, falling to the pavement. She lifts her powerful leg as if to stomp his head. "You picked the wrong house, scumbag."

"It's me." He rips off his hat and sunglasses.

Her foot suspends. "Dapino?"

He smiles. "Stressful commute?"

She sets her foot to the pavement, her hands on her hips. "Thought you were some low-rent burglar."

"It's okay."

"It's not. You're an escaped prisoner. On my property. What the hell are you doing here?" She looks over her shoulder.

"I was careful. No neighbors saw me."

"How do I know that?"

"The cops would already be here."

"Maybe they're on the way. About to roll up on a federal agent kibitzing with a fugitive. How am I supposed to explain that to my boss?"

"Let's get out of the driveway, go inside."

"I should be getting my cuffs out instead."

"If you want to arrest me, fine. That's a risk I was willing to take coming here. You're my only hope."

"You think I have the power to just snap my fingers and make your legal troubles go away?"

"No."

"Then what were you hoping for?"

"You must know I wasn't behind Jordana's kidnap. I'm going to find her."

"We're already looking for her."

"The chances of locating her go up if I'm looking too. All I need from you is intel to point me in the right direction on the search. Case info you already have access to."

She laughs. "So you're asking me to leak confidential details about an ongoing investigation . . . to the main suspect?"

"That about sums it up."

She sniffs him. "By the way, you smell like ass."

"That's not an ass. It's a sewer. Long story."

"I don't want to hear it." She grunts. "Fine, Dapino. I suppose the likelihood of Jordana coming home alive improves if you're on this too. But I'm giving myself an out if I need it."

"What do you mean?"

She clutches his hair and tears out a few strands.

"Ah," he says. "What was that for?"

# TWELVE

Tommy sits on a brown-leather couch in Wichita's wood-paneled den, a framed photo of a 1990s version of her on the wall at a powerlifting competition, veins bulging from her neck during a squat. She's been elsewhere in the house the last few minutes. During which she put on music, a Sting song emitting from a speaker at low volume.

She reenters the den. In one hand a Ziploc bag of Tommy's yanked-out hair, in the other a blue folder. She sits on an armchair across from him, pats the folder. "What you want is in here."

He stoops forward, extends his hand. She doesn't pass it to him.

"Before I give you anything," she says, "you must agree to my terms."

He leans back. "Shoot."

"You use this information to bring Jordana home safe, good things happen for you. She'll make a statement about what really transpired. Charges against you will be dropped. Technically you are guilty of jailbreak, but no DA in sound mind would pursue that against an innocent escapee."

"You're forgetting the most important thing. I'll get my girlfriend back."

"Of course. And I'll get back a dear friend. You ready for the bad?"

He nods at the Ziploc bag. "Let me guess. You're going to tell me I'm not using the right conditioner?"

"That isn't funny, Dapino."

"I'm sorry."

"You will be in some serious shit if you don't comprehend what I'm about to communicate."

"My ears are open. Thank you for helping me. Means a lot you think I'm innocent."

"Don't thank me yet. If you pursue the intel in this folder, yet fail to find Jordana, eventually the cops will find you. After they lock you back up, they'll probe everything you did on the outside. And likely tie you to the information in here. Wonder how you got it. And under no circumstances could they learn I voluntarily gave it."

"You really think I'd snitch on you?"

"No. But if a public camera captured you anywhere in Sorrento Valley, they could connect the dots. So if you get arrested, you'll also be charged for breaking and entering. And theft."

"Where did I break into? What did I steal?"

"Nowhere and nothing. But I'm planning on proactively covering my ass. You get busted, I'm saying someone snuck into my house and swiped a file off my computer." She jiggles the bag of hair. "Just got to bust a window and sprinkle a couple of these guys by it before the CSI team shows up."

He rubs his forehead. "That's icy."

"That's my offer. Which you still have an opportunity to pass on. You can turn yourself in now and avoid the possibility of the extra charges. Or I give you the file and you face more years in prison."

"Give me the damn folder." She grins, hands it to him. He flips through the pages. "So who's the asshole in the ski mask who decked my girlfriend?"

"No name on him yet. But we feel he's connected to a case she was working."

"She never talks about active investigations with me. I know she'd been busy lately, but not on what."

"The yogurt attendant got a quick look at the van's plate. Didn't recall its number, but mentioned it was colorful. Probably not California's basic white."

"Which state?"

"She couldn't tell."

"A lot of states have colorful plates. How does that help?"

"Did Jordana tell you she went on a work-related road trip earlier in the week?"

"Yeah. But not to where."

Wichita taps a few buttons on her phone, presents her screen to Tommy. "Here."

He peers at a stock photo of a Nevada license plate.

It's quite colorful.

He places his foot on his knee. "What was she up to in Nevada?"

"Everything she documented is in the folder. But we doubt it's the complete picture. She was probably waiting to close a few gaps before writing up a full report. Before she could, she vanished."

"I'll retrace her steps."

"We sent a couple agents to do just that yesterday.

But I'm warning you, they hit a wall."

He closes the folder and stands. "I guess that means it's time for a hammer."

# THIRTEEN

From the back of a cab, Tommy gazes at the Nevada desert along the I-15. Dark, quiet, and still, as if an extension of the night. Before he departed from Wichita's, he took a shower while she stopped at Walmart to pick him up a new burner phone. He calls Josh on it.

"Hello?" Josh says.

"FYI, you may notice a somewhat high charge from the San Diego Taxi Company on that credit card you loaned me."

"T. Thank God. Don't worry about the Cap One. I know you're good for the dough. What's this number? You're not calling from jail, are you?"

"No. But I just crossed state lines. Definitely don't want to end up there now."

"Jordana's in a different state?"

"I don't know where specifically. But someone here might. Rural Nevada. You've got to see it out here, dude. Nothing but sand for miles. Then a little town with about six houses. Then nothing but sand again. She came out here five days ago to interview a suspect in an FBI case. Right after, she gets kidnapped."

"Who the hell did she interview?"

"Apparently never found the suspect. Spoke to the mother."

"This guy a heavy hitter? Drug kingpin, something like that?"

"Nothing like that. Not a guy. Some girl. Young, twenty-one. No priors."

"What's the FBI after her for, shoplifting lip gloss at the mall?"

"I wish. She somehow found her way into the blackmail business. Even if she's not dangerous herself, seems she's working with someone who is. Looks like she's the lure in some honeytrap operation."

"A what?"

"An attractive girl baits an unsuspecting man into a compromising financial situation. In this case, the sucker was an aerospace executive from Indiana. He goes to a convention in Vegas. Afterward, his wife notices fifty grand missing from their bank account."

"That's some high-end honey."

"The money was converted to cryptocurrency, then sent to some untraceable recipient. Wife asks him what the hell is going on, husband claims some cyberthief must've lifted his banking password. They go to the police, who pass them to the FBI. Jordana apparently just worked a cyber case, so the agent in Indiana consulted her. Jordana didn't buy the husband's story."

"Why not?"

"She looked into his stay in Vegas. Got access to surveillance footage from his hotel. The camera systems in these casinos are nuts. You can upload a photo of a face and get back a recording of everywhere the person stepped foot across the entire property. During a time window the guy said he was at some business dinner, Jordana spots him at a bar flirting with a girl thirty years younger than him, and confronted him about it. He cracked. Came clean. Said the girl got dirt on him, then some man strongarmed him over the phone for the money."

"Huh. Can't believe the idiot made the mistake of paying them from a joint banking account."

"Maybe they gave him a deadline, was shook up, rushed. Anyway, now he's out the fifty, plus whatever the divorce will cost."

"Scary. Guy builds a life with a woman over decades. All it takes is some random hot girl to bat her eyes at him at a bar and it all comes crumbling down."

"I . . . that's his problem. I don't know. Facial recognition software put a name on the honey trapper. Alexa Thoss. She can lead me to Jordana."

"What'd her mom say?"

"Don't know. Jordana stopped at her house. That's where her write-up ends. I'll have to find out what went down myself."

A moment. "You sure this is a good idea, T?"

"This is the only idea I've got."

"Jordana poked around these people. And ended up in the back of a van. Who says the same won't happen to you?"

The cab exits onto a winding road, the twinkle of headlights on the freeway fading behind Tommy, no other cars going this way.

"Get some rest," Tommy says. "I'll hit you up tomorrow." He ends the call.

According to Google Maps, Alexa Thoss's mother

lives eight minutes away in a town called Willince. But showing up past midnight would seem suspicious. Tommy will need to wait till morning.

"Just drop me off in town," he tells the cabbie.

The taxi's headlights cut through country darkness onto Willince's main street, providing a dim visibility of the town's businesses, some windows sealed with plywood. The ones that appear operational are all closed at this hour. *GROCERIES. FUEL. GUNS & AMMO.*

The cabbie rolls to a halt in the barren street. Tommy exits into the dry heat, waves goodbye.

He sits on the dusty ground, leans against the side of an abandoned shop. Then looks up at the desert moon. When it goes down and the sun comes up, the third day since Jordana's disappearance will begin. The next time the moon is out, the seventy-two hours will be expired. He has till tomorrow to rescue his girlfriend from the jaws of this enigma.

He struggles to fall asleep. When he does, a cave comes to him in his dream. In it, naked Jordana floats on a dark bed of water, flowers over her eyes. Her skin pale. Tommy opens his mouth to say something to her. He isn't certain what.

# FOURTEEN

Tommy walks Willince's main road sweating from the brow, almost ninety degrees in the desert at eight AM. Locals on the sidewalk eyeball the stranger in the tiger shirt. A man chewing tobacco spits on the ground a couple feet in front of his path. Tommy stares into his eyes. The man and his friend smirk. Tommy steps around the gooey wad.

He covers a mile or so. Then turns right onto an unpaved road. Soon he comes to the trailer home owned by Alexa Thoss's mom, Lucy, an old pickup truck and sedan in front, a rusty swing set in back among bushes spiking out of the sand.

He knocks on the door. No answer. He glimpses the front window, polka-dot-patterned curtains over it. A bug lands on his ear. He shakes his head. The largest fly he's ever seen shoots off him.

Maybe he can get a look through a back window. He veers toward the trailer's rear, the overhead buzz of the bug sounding like a WWII bomber plane. Above it he hears the front door open.

He glances over his shoulder. Someone turns the trailer's corner. Not the middle-aged woman he was expecting. A male, early twenties, blond buzzcut. His tan shirt is so worn out it's almost see-through.

"What you doing on this property?" the kid asks. He isn't big, about five eight, one forty, but looks strong, the wiry athleticism of a varsity wrestler.

Tommy holds up his hands to indicate no harm intended. "Is Mrs. Thoss home?"

"Who askin'?"

A moment. "I'm a reporter."

"Dressed like an asshole who sells tickets at the zoo?"

"Our office culture is on the zestier side."

"What my mom gonna be in the news for?"

"Not sure if she told you, but an FBI agent went missing in California and your mother—"

"Two fed dickheads showed up yesterday grilling her on it. She know the same thing 'bout it today she did then." The kid spits. "Nothin'."

"That's all right. For my article, I only need to learn about the interaction she had with Jordana."

The kid steps closer to Tommy. "What paper it for?"

"*The San Diego Herald.*" The fly lands on Tommy's nose. He swats at it, slapping his own face. "Are all the bugs out here that big? Jesus."

The kid nods at the dusty road in front of the mobile home. "I didn't see no car out there. You walked to Willince from San Diego?"

"Funny story actually. When they say get your oil

changed every five thousand miles, there's a distinct reason. To prevent you from breaking down and hitch-hiking with a truck driver who enjoys singing along to Mariah Carey albums at the top of his lungs."

The kid slips a thumb into his jeans' pocket. "I reckon it's time you find another truck driver to take you the way you came."

"It was a lot of trouble for me to get all the way out here." Tommy paces toward the front door. "I only need a couple minutes of your mom's time."

"Well, she don't need none of yours." The kid grasps Tommy's forearm.

"I'm not looking for any trouble."

"I am if you don't leave our property."

Tommy doesn't budge. The kid shoves him toward the road.

"Watch yourself," Tommy says.

"Watch this." The kid dives at his shins. Their bodies drop onto the hard-packed sand. They wrestle, Tommy's sunglasses falling off.

*Bachoon.* A blasting noise echoes through the sky. They freeze. A middle-aged woman stands in the doorway with a shotgun. Frizzy brown hair gray at the roots, a smoker's complexion, a drinker's midsection.

"He's just some reporter, Mom," the kid says. "Was trying to stop him from bothering you."

She aims the weapon at Tommy. "No, child. He is not a reporter."

# FIFTEEN

The inside of Lucy Thoss's trailer is cluttered with cardboard boxes of hoarded items, condiment packages, batteries, crease-cornered *Cosmopolitan* magazines dating back a decade. Her son duct-tapes Tommy's ankles to a metal folding chair, his wrists already bound behind his back, his Yankees cap crooked.

A Marlboro dangling from her lip, Lucy holds her eyes and her shotgun on Tommy. "I went to school with this boy named Herby," she says. "And he taught me a lesson I haven't forgotten after all these years. Take a guess at what it involved."

"How not to run out of ketchup?"

"A comedian." She squeezes one of her breasts. "The lesson involved these."

"Should I go in the other room for this, Mama?" her son asks.

"No honey. I want you to listen too. It's an important lesson. In ninth grade, Herby accused me of stuffing my bra with Kleenex. Do these look like they're stuffed?"

Tommy doesn't reply, peering down at the shaggy brown carpet.

"Huh?" she blurts.

"No . . . they're quite authentic in appearance."

"For damn near a month I stared at them in the mirror every night. Wondered if something was wrong with them, if they puffed under my shirt all weird like tissues would. I couldn't see anything off. But I assumed Herby could. And that ate at me."

"He sounds like a big jerk," her son says.

"He was. But that wasn't his only problem." She focuses on Tommy. "Summer when we was fifteen, my friend and him got to making out in the closet at a party. And she pulled down Herby's jeans. And you know what she found?" Lucy holds up her pinky finger. "You see the lesson?"

"Herby should've picked a closet with darker lighting," Tommy says.

"My tits weren't small. His cock was. If someone accuses you of something, good chance they're guilty of it themself." She has a drag of her cigarette. "And that's exactly what you did to me today."

"Whoa. I didn't accuse you of anything. I was—"

"You showed up here asking about that girl disappearing. Same thing as the two FBI men. You come out here to pin this on me? I didn't take her. You did."

"Hold on up," her son says. "Him? He the kidnapper?"

"Believe it, child. I was curious after the FBI men left yesterday, so went on the internet and typed in Jordana Quick. News article comes up saying her boyfriend was arrested for kidnap something or other. And escaped from jail. So I'm even more curious, type in his name next. Thomas Dapino. See his picture." Lucy runs her finger down Tommy's cheek. "I said to myself, Lord, that's a nice-looking man. I wasn't forgetting this face."

She sets the barrel of the shotgun on Tommy's seat, a metal-on-metal thud. It's aimed at his crotch.

His breathing picks up. She taps the gun on the chair, a vibration running up his hamstrings. Taps again. Continues for about half a minute.

"I'm calling the police on you," she says. "And you're going back to jail. But before I do, I'm giving you a chance to tell me exactly what you came here to do. If I get a believable answer, I won't blow your package off."

Her son rubs his forehead, mumbles, "Oh boy."

"He'll be even less of a boy than Herby if he doesn't tell me the truth."

"I didn't kidnap my girlfriend," Tommy says in a rushed voice. "I don't think you did either. But whoever did is still out there. He's extremely dangerous. And my guess is your daughter is mixed up with him. I came here for information to find out who he is. Then stop him before he does more harm."

The son asks, "You're saying my little sister, she in harm's way?"

"When Jordana came here to ask about her, I'm sure she didn't give much context, the other FBI agents either. That's how feds operate. Everything is on a need-to-know basis. The real reason Jordana needed Alexa's current address is because she's wanted for a crime."

Lucy and her son look at each other, then back at Tommy. "Alexa is many things," she says, "but ain't a criminal."

"She somehow got involved with a man who is. She could be in way over her head. And not even know it. When's the last you spoke to her?"

"Not since she left me and Kurt for that Devil's playground Las Vegas. Right after she turned twenty-one. Almost four months back."

"We tried calling, texting," the son, who must be Kurt, says. "She don't respond."

"You spend time in the land of the Devil," Lucy says, "you eventually getting burnt. Maybe Alexa deserves this trouble she's in. Maybe it'll teach her a lesson."

"You can't learn a lesson if you're dead," Tommy says.

"This man she apparently workin' with, he have a reason to . . . kill her?" Kurt asks.

"Not yet. But that can change. He beat the shit out of my girlfriend. Men who're violent to women tend to be unstable. Doesn't take much for them to view an ally as an enemy."

"This smells like a pot of lies," Lucy says.

"Maybe I am lying. You can't know for certain. But if I'm not, wouldn't you want someone to make sure Alexa is okay? If I can bring down the real kidnapper, he'd be out of her life."

"And we're supposed to believe some two-face scared of a fly gonna bring down this big, bad man?" Kurt asks.

"I wasn't scared of that fly. I was just taken aback by its girth." Tommy looks around the shabby trailer. "No offense, hiring a PI to track down Alexa is probably out of your budget. I would know. I am one. If you let me go, let me back on the trail, you'll be getting my services for free. Worst case, I fail. Costs you nothing.

Best case I save her life."

"If you're not lying about this mess," Lucy says, "it's one Alexa got herself into. Let her get herself out."

A few seconds of silence. Kurt scratches his head. "I don't know, Mama. I don't like this dipshit Dapino any more than you. But seems we got nothin' to lose letting him go out there and see to it Alexa all right. You always said it yourself, that girl don't have much brains. We can't leave her out there all on her own, right?"

A moment. Lucy inhales a long drag from her cigarette.

# SIXTEEN

A wooden crucifix hangs on the trailer's wall, more anguish in this Jesus' expression than on others Tommy's seen over the years. His wrists and ankles no longer taped, he sits on the sofa beside Lucy while Kurt calls Alexa. A half-minute passes.

"Huh," Kurt says.

"What?" Tommy asks.

"I got like some weird message from the phone company. Number not in service no more."

"Eh. That isn't good. Makes sense though. When she started dabbling in activities not fully legal, she probably ditched her registered phone, been communicating on a burner. Why the feds have had such a hard time locating her." Tommy leans forward. "Her father. Maybe she's in communication with him. Maybe he'd have an address for her in Vegas."

Lucy taps her Marlboro on the rim of an empty beer can used as an ashtray. "Somewhat strange what I was attracted to back then. I had plenty of options in those days, but I chose to have not one but two children with a man who showed zero sign of a child-raising skillset."

"Where is he—"

"He was a musician." She laughs, shakes her head. "He sucked at it. But thought he was great, was totally full of himself. Heroin binges. Drank a shit ton. Yelled all the time. Cheated on me." She pushes a loose strand of hair from her eyes. "Did a lot worse than that too."

"Sorry . . . to hear that. How can I contact—"

"But before he left, I did love fucking his brains out." She puffs the cigarette. "Funny how that works, isn't it?"

"Mama has Jesus now," Kurt says. "She don't need no man."

Lucy smiles, says to Tommy, "My ex wouldn't know where Alexa is. He's long out of his daughter's life. With all those drugs he was into, he's probably long out of his too."

"What about friends from town she may have kept in touch with?"

"I guess she has a couple. But never brought them around here. Me or Kurt wouldn't know anything about them."

Tommy folds his arms. "Fair enough. So Jordana comes by. Asks where Alexa is. You tell her no clue. Then what?"

"Alexa's room. She wanted to look around."

"She find anything helpful?"

Lucy shrugs. "Didn't say one way or the other."

"She comes out, then what?"

"She left."

"Did she leave fast, like she had somewhere else to go, or did she hang around, ask you any more questions?"

"Gave me her card, then left pretty much right away."

Tommy nods. "I need to check out the room."

"I'll tell you the same thing I told your girlfriend and the two feds yesterday. Look all you want, but no walking off with anything. When something finds its way into my home that good money was spent on, I prefer it stay in my home. Don't know when we got so wasteful as a people."

"I won't take a thing, Mrs. Thoss."

She points at a door beside Kurt's. Tommy enters the room, a dog inside resting on the floor. A poster of a black heart on the wall. He peeks under the bed. Nothing. He opens the closet, twenty or so hangers with no clothes. Then the top dresser drawer, empty. Just a few socks in the second drawer, nothing the third.

He wanders to a desk, a single pen on it. No computer. No tablet. An attached bookshelf. He glimpses the book spines. All of them about self-improvement, all standing vertical but the one on the end, lying on its back. He opens it, notices a pen scribble on the inside of the front cover, *Rose Lg 7*.

"Hey," he says toward the den. "Mind looking at this?"

In a few seconds, Lucy meanders inside with a fresh Marlboro. She eyes Tommy from toe to head. "I don't mind looking at all."

"Know what this might mean?" he asks, presenting *Rose Lg 7* to her and Kurt.

"Nope," she says.

Kurt shakes his head.

"Seven large roses?" Tommy says.

"I don't know who she would've bought roses for," Lucy says. "Certainly not her mother."

Tommy scrutinizes the text. "Is she right-handed or left-?"

"Left," she says.

He studies the text a bit longer. "Her letters bunch to the right and angle up."

"That supposed to mean something?"

"It's as if the surface she was writing on was moving. Like she had the pen in her left hand, but her right wasn't steadying the book below."

"So?"

"Her right hand was occupied while she was jotting something down. Meaning she was probably on her phone, taking a note from whoever she was speaking to. Any idea who that could've been?"

"Like I said, the couple friends she had weren't—"

"Maybe it wasn't a friend." He points at the 7 in the book. "This could mean seven o'clock. An appointment she called to make. What sort of appointments did she go on?"

"She got her hair done every few weeks at the shop Betsy Ann Mayfield runs in the back of her house. Always in the afternoons, not seven AM or PM."

"What about a doctor?"

"That child's been sick about twice her whole life. Nothing more than a cold."

He crosses his arms. "Before she moved to Vegas, did she ask you for any money?"

"Her, me, and Kurt got into a big fight right before she left. We warned her against living amongst all that filth. But she didn't listen. I certainly wasn't going to support her with any good money. And she had enough sense not to ask."

"Then I'm sure she needed work in Vegas right away. Seven o'clock." He smiles. "A job interview."

"Huh."

On his phone he Googles "Rose Lg Las Vegas." A handful of results come up for rose-colored LG cellphones for sale in Las Vegas shops. Among them is a link to the website of a place called Rose Lounge.

He visits it and shows his screen to Lucy. "Could've applied here as a waitress."

She gazes at a website image of an attractive girl in a Rose Lounge tank top holding a drink tray. "Getting paid to objectify her own body. Yes, that is a job my daughter would take."

"The two FBI agents yesterday maybe didn't see this note in the book or did and just dismissed it. But Jordana doesn't miss anything. When she hurried out of here, good chance she came to the same conclusion as me about Rose Lounge and headed there. The staff could have information. I need to talk to them."

"Las Vegas different from Willince in a lot more areas than morals. It's crowded. Cameras everywhere. A fugitive with a sexy face like you shows up, some Nosy Norma or Ned will recognize him. Tsk, tsk, tsk."

Tommy deflates against the desk. "Hmm."

"Looks like I'll have to go with him," Kurt says.

# SEVENTEEN

Tommy squints in the sun, even brighter since he's been outside last. He puts his recovered shades back on. The scuffle with Kurt must've scratched the lenses, his view of the world a tad blurred.

 Kurt steps out of the trailer with a duffel bag. He hugs Lucy in the doorway, says, "Be home soon, Mama."

She kisses his forehead. "Stay safe, my boy."

The dog, a collie, runs outside, jumps on Kurt. "Hey Buckles," he says, dropping to his knees. "You gonna be good when I'm gone?"

"Nice-looking animal," Tommy says.

"Neighbor up the road is one of them breeders," Kurt says, rubbing Buckles's back. "Gave us him at a real good price couple years ago. Could be in shows, all that. Great lineage."

"What do you mean, lineage?"

"Breeder finds a girl dog and boy dog with good genes. Puts 'em together. And then you get a really high chance the pups get those good genes coming down to 'em. Nice coat. Nice teeth. Good temperament. Breeder says temperament means like the mind, like the dog don't go crazy on you."

Whistling, Kurt walks to his Chevy pickup, scattered dents along the side and back. A cigarette between her fingers, a leer in her eyes, Lucy waves goodbye to Tommy, then disappears inside the trailer, the screen door smacking shut.

He treads the sandy yard toward the truck. A snake slithers across the terrain a few feet in front of him. It looks at him for a second, then vanishes into the spiky bushes.

Tommy climbs in the passenger seat next to Kurt, who tosses his duffel bag in the back. "What you got in there?" Tommy asks.

Kurt unzips it. "Man's other best friend."

Tommy peeks at the glisten of a gun. "What're you planning on doing with that, cowboy?"

"Me and Alexa may not get along that great. But she's still my sister. And if some slimy blackmailer thinks about hurting her, I got it in my mind to blow his head straight off."

"I appreciate the gusto, but try not to do anything too brash out there. Could . . . complicate things."

"Coming from a maniac all over the internet for bustin' outta jail?"

Tommy drums his thigh with his thumb. Kurt starts the truck. The engine sounds like loose change clanging around under the hood. They roll onto the unpaved road.

"We'll need a recent photo of your sister to show

around at Rose Lounge," Tommy says. "Got anything?"

One hand on the wheel, Kurt fishes his phone from his pocket with the other. He scrolls through it, presents a picture of Alexa. "This'll work?"

She is at a nighttime bonfire party, glancing over her shoulder at the camera as if the photo were spontaneous, strands of her mid-back-length blond hair in motion from the turn of her head, the lids of her blue eyes a touch closed, on her lips a trace of a smirk.

A pang of guilt in Tommy's chest. He tells himself he's supposed to be in love with Jordana, that some image of a stranger shouldn't make him feel the way it does.

Kurt must be able to discern the picture has an effect on him, because he says, "Yeah, she's pretty, I know." A moment. "Mama was pretty too when she was young. Not like Alexa, but prettier than most. She'd always tell Alexa she got lucky she at least got that."

"Maybe your mom is wrong about her. Maybe she has more going on for her than how she looks. Not many people are sharp enough to evade the FBI."

Kurt turns onto the main road. Waves to a local on the sidewalk. "Well, I guess sometimes Mama could be hard on her. I think because how much my daddy liked Alexa. Mama sure didn't appreciate all the attention he gave her. One morning she was hollerin' at him over it. Got so mad this big-ole vein ran right up her forehead. She threw a plate against the wall, broke to little pieces just about everywhere. My daddy packed a suitcase right then and there, left . . . and never came back."

"I've heard of couples getting divorced because a dad showed no interest in his kids. Never because a dad showed too much."

"Didn't make much sense to me neither."

"What did he and your sister do that got to her so much?"

"While ago. I remember Alexa really liked this picture book when she was 'bout eight or nine, though. It was about a dinosaur or something like that. And my daddy would go into her room and read it to her at night now and then. Past our bedtime. And he'd stay in there real late. The mornings after he read to her, I remember Mama would yell. And Alexa would cry a lot."

Tommy nods. "Ah." He lets out a long exhale. "Well, you're a good brother for helping me find her. I used to have a sister. She was caught up in some rough stuff. I was too . . . messed up in those days to help her. We lost her. But Alexa might have a shot at a second chance."

"Look Dapino, I may still not trust you, but that handwriting thing you came up with back there . . . that was nice stuff."

"Thanks, cowboy."

"Me? I dropped out of eighth grade. I ain't never dreaming up no smart idea just from seeing some words scribbled down someplace. What I can promise you is I've got enough piss and vinegar to fill up a bathtub. And that's gotta be worth somethin'."

Tommy grins. "It's worth a lot more than school."

An inkling of a smile on Kurt. He flips on a country-music station.

After a few dozen miles, the Las Vegas Strip emerges on the horizon. "Can't believe God let this disease spread in a place as holy as a desert," Kurt says.

Giant towers compete for sky space. Massive electric billboards herald fancy shows, fancy meals, fancy people.

In crevices among the glitz is the city's other side. Disillusioned-looking men stumbling out of casinos in last night's clothing, low-end street performers in tattered costumes, hookers with druggie bodies adjusting their tits in the reflections of shops' glass fronts.

Soon Tommy and Kurt pull into the parking lot of Rose Lounge.

# EIGHTEEN

Tommy waits in the pickup while Kurt asks about Alexa inside Rose Lounge. Across the street, Tommy notices three tents, a half-dozen homeless people hanging around. Two of the men, one shirtless, play chess.

A vibration against Tommy's leg. A call from a 718 area code. He recognizes the rest of the number. "Crap," he says. Then answers. "Hey Ma."

"Jail?"

"Ma, I can—"

"Then a jailbreak?"

"Did you get this number from Josh?"

"Police after you with all those guns? If you escaped jail, they'll shoot you right in the face. They're allowed."

"Not sure about that. But it's all right. I didn't get

shot in the face."

"Not yet. Oh Tommy. You don't tell your mother about this?"

"I didn't want to freak you out. Looks like Josh already accomplished that."

"Josh is such a nice boy. He texts me on my birthday. Every year. Even when you and me weren't talking for a while. He's worried just as much as me. So this number is how I reach you now?"

"If any police ask if you spoke to me, say no, and do not give them this number."

"Can you believe this? Okay. The cops contacting me about my son the fugitive. I thought it was a joke at first. Like when you and Josh were kids and convinced me the eyes on my Virgin Mary painting were following me around the living room."

"That was a good one."

"So what is happening out there, Tommy? Are you okay? Are you eating?"

"I'm fine." He rubs his forehead. "So, now that you're on the phone, I've actually got a question I was planning on asking you."

"What?"

"That watch grandpa left me. The Patek Philippe. Is it . . . fake?"

A pause. "Why're you asking me that?"

"Doesn't matter. I was so young when he died, I didn't really know him. You did. Would he do something like that? Give me a phony watch?"

A sigh from her. "Your dad, God knows where he is these days, is a . . . unique man. His dad was too. Both of them charismatic. But also . . . I don't know."

"What?"

"Selfish. Best I could describe it."

"I know dad . . . wasn't the best husband. But I

always thought grandpa was just a nice, solid guy."

"Maybe when he was older and slowed down. But one Christmas, your aunt had a few spritzers in her, and told me he flaunted his mistresses right in front of your grandma. He'd go through her closet and give these women her old clothes as gifts, take them to the dry cleaner first, put them in a box, pretend they were new. He was well aware your grandma could run into them in town, see them wearing her sweater or hat or whatever. Apparently happened three times."

"Huh."

"Your father at least had the respect to sneak around behind my back. But he had other issues. When you were a kid, remember he said he had that job as a personal trainer at a gym?"

"Empire Fitness."

"Made up. I found out his sole source of income during that stretch was robbing meat trucks in the West Village. I confronted him about it. I go if you steal from the wrong guy, maybe a connected guy, you know, what if he sends some muscle to the house looking for you? Where your son and daughter live. He told me to take a Xanax, then met up with his friends to get drunk, didn't show back up until two PM the next day."

"Huh."

"Look, don't get me wrong, he could be charming. Nice smile too. Why I married him. Your grandfather too. But most of their good qualities were just ... on the surface. When it came down to going the extra mile to take care of the people close to them, they ... quit on you. So would it surprise me if your grandfather passed you down a watch knowing it was fake? No, not at all."

He scratches his cheek. "Thanks ... uh, for being

honest with me. Anyway, you have to come out here and meet Jordana. When this is all over."

"She sounds like a lovely girl."

"Classy. That's what she is. She might be the one. Let me tell you. She'd be a great mom."

"Well, don't give her a ring until you're sure she's the one. For life. Last thing she needs is some guy to eat up the rest of her twenties, then thirties. Then abandon her in her forties."

"Jesus. I was trying to talk about something positive. Why do you immediately go there?"

"What do they do again, her family? Make soda?"

"Wine. Velatti. It's in all the stores. You've seen it."

"Speaking of stores, how're you eating if you can't go into public places like groceries? Maybe I can overnight you something from Franco's market."

Kurt exits Rose Lounge.

"Thanks, but don't worry about it, Ma," Tommy says. "I got to go."

"Call me if you need anything. Love you."

"Love you too. Bye." He hangs up.

Kurt climbs into the pickup. He sets a small square object on the center console. A napkin with the bar's logo, a long-stemmed red rose with pronounced thorns. Written on it in pen is an address in Henderson, one town over.

"Your sister is in Henderson?" Tommy asks.

"No. But a guy there knows where to find her."

"What guy?"

"So I go in and show Alexa's photo to the bartender. He said she worked there when she first got to town. Don't know where she was now. The manager overhears us talking, tells me she quit in her first month, ain't seen her since. But knows someone who might be able to help. So he calls this guy. And the guy gave him that there address. Said I should stop by and he'll answer any questions."

"Who is he to Alexa? How does he know where she is but the FBI doesn't?"

"Asked the manager the same thing. He said this man met her at the bar right before she quit. They was flirting and all. Mama taught us the importance of staying pure. I listened. But Alexa, I don't know. Manager thinks maybe they dating or something now."

Tommy stares at the address. "A boyfriend. I guess he would know where she was. That worked out, huh? Nice job, cowboy."

Kurt starts the engine, enters the address on the napkin into his GPS, and pulls out of the lot. He hums a song.

"Glad you don't like Vegas," Tommy says. "You won't be disappointed when nobody in town offers you a music gig."

"Ah, screw off. I'm just like doing a little tune to pass the time. That was nothing. I wasn't trying to sound good."

"So, if you wanted, you could sound good?"

"Oh yeah."

"Let me hear."

"No."

"If you were any good, you'd show me."

"I don't have to show you shit."

"I know. But if you don't, I'll assume you're a shitty singer."

"What's that, some city-slicker mind trick? I ain't doing it."

"Fine."

Neither speaks for about two minutes. Then Kurt begins singing "Lay Down Sally" by Eric Clapton. He's not bad.

Tommy slaps his thigh to the rhythm. "There it is."

Kurt sings a bit more, then says in his regular voice, "That's all you gettin'."

Tommy applauds.

In about a half hour they're far from the modern architecture of Vegas, on a road bordered by mountains. Long lengths of wooden fencing up ahead surround a large plot of land. Kurt slows to a stop.

"We're at the address?" Tommy asks.

Kurt double-checks the napkin and GPS. "Yep."

No people in sight, just a couple dozen horses roaming about the hardscrabble, a farmhouse tucked a few hundred feet back.

"Country girl moves to Vegas to date a horse farmer?" Tommy asks. "Don't you have guys like that back in Willince?"

"Maybe the manager was wrong. She ain't dating this guy. Maybe she work for him. Like got a job hosing down stables."

"She quit waitressing at a popular bar to operate a hose?"

"Only one way to find out." Kurt steps out of the pickup. "I'll talk to him." He closes the door.

Arms folded, Tommy watches him walk toward the farmhouse. A few of the horses stop trotting, stare at the human.

Pinches on Tommy's face. *Bachaa*, a loud, echoing noise. The pickup's windshield, a hole in it. The driver's headrest demolished. The horses neigh.

Tommy ducks, glances through the cracked windshield. A few hundred feet away a gray van is parked on the roadside sand. Beside it a tall man in a ski mask. A rifle in his grip.

"Get down," Tommy screams toward Kurt.

Confusion streaks Kurt's face. His back to the rifleman, he must not know what's happening.

Tommy opens the door, scrambles outside. Dives into Kurt.

*Bachaa*, another gunshot. Tommy slams Kurt to the ground under the bullet, which obliterates a fencepost.

Tommy's body slides against the dry terrain, a sharp rock digging into his forearm. He grabs Kurt by the elbow, drags him toward the pickup. Through a cloud of dust, the shooter fixes his aim on them.

*Pralink*. The bullet smacks into the truck's side no more than a foot from them. Tommy and Kurt crawl to its rear.

*Sutoof*. A shot tears through the front-left tire, air hissing from it.

"What the hell?" a male voice screams.

A man in overalls grasping a shotgun emerges from the farmhouse, looks toward the rifleman. Who jumps in the gray van. Speeds in the opposite direction of the pickup. At this distance, in the glare of the sun, Tommy can't discern a plate number.

"What the fuck was that?" Kurt blurts, sand stuck to the sweat on his forehead.

"Let's follow the van," Tommy says. He dashes into the pickup from the passenger side, blood oozing from the cut on his forearm.

Kurt fumbles in through the driver's side. Starts the engine. He drives the way the van did. But the old pickup, now with a flat tire, clunks ahead at a slow pace. The van no longer visible.

Tommy kicks the door panel. "He's gone."

"What now?"

"You got a spare tire?"

"Yeah."

"Let's hurry up and change it. Get back to Rose

Lounge before the manager bolts. And find out why this son of a bitch just sent us into an execution."

# NINETEEN

Its tire changed, the pickup zooms toward Rose Lounge. Kurt's hands tremble against the wheel. Tommy reaches to the backseat, drops of blood spilling off his arm. He unzips the duffel bag, pulls out the gun, and sets it on the console. "Don't let the manager play dumb."

Kurt gulps. "I only packed that as a just-in-case sort of thing."

"We've now arrived at a case."

Kurt says in a soft voice, "I, uh . . . well . . . I don't really know how to use it. Never fired it."

Tommy surveys him. In his worked-up condition, Kurt can't pull this off. "What does the manager look like?" Tommy asks.

"Like five eleven. Older, 'bout my mom's age. Hawaiian shirt. Why?" Kurt turns into the Rose

Lounge parking lot.

Tommy sticks the gun in the waist of his jeans, flaps his shirt over it. "Keep the truck running."

Kurt holds his foot on the brake. "You can't go in there. There're . . . customers. Cameras. You gonna get spotted, then the cops—"

Tommy hops out of the pickup. Storms toward Rose Lounge's door. Shoves it open. A mural of a thorny red rose on the wall, black-and-white tile dancefloor, female singer in a satin dress belting out "Cupid" by Sam Cooke.

Tommy eyes the crowd in the low lighting. Around two dozen patrons, among them five girls in matching "Bride's Babes" tank tops and a sixth in a tiara. A middle-aged guy in a Hawaiian shirt leans over the bar with a flirty grin, asks them, "Want to see a magic trick? One of you, pick a number between one and ten."

Tommy stomps toward them. A customer gapes at the blood crisscrossing his forearm. Tommy reaches through the bachelorette party, grasps the manager by the hair, and smashes his head into the counter.

Scattered gasps. Tommy hops to the other side of the bar and flips the manager to face him. A lump swells on the man's forehead. The singer continues the song without a hitch.

"Who was waiting for us at the horse farm?" Tommy shouts.

"What horse farm?"

Tommy punches his gut. "The address you just wrote for my friend on the napkin."

The manager wheezes. "The blond kid?"

"Yes asshole. Who tried to shoot us?"

"Back away from him," a large Black bouncer says.

Tommy lifts the back of his shirt, revealing the

gun. "This doesn't concern you, captain."

The bouncer raises his hands, backpedals. Guests sprint past him toward the exit.

One of the bachelorette girls says into her phone, "Some nutso guy with a gun. Rose Lounge. Attacking like the manager dude." Her voice fades as she approaches the door.

Won't be long till the cops show up.

Tommy says to the manager, "You do magic, huh? For the best tricks, the magician dies if he screws up, drowns in the water if he doesn't get out of the strait-jacket, that sort of thing." Tommy presses the gun to his head. "Trick me into believing you."

The manager whimpers. "I . . . just wrote down the address he said. Didn't—"

"He? Who's he?"

"I don't know his name. He tried to shoot you? What? Why?"

The manager seems surprised. Maybe his ignorance is real. Or maybe he's just a good actor. Either way, Tommy doesn't have the time to wait here and find out.

He yanks him to his feet, thrusts the gun into his rib. "Walk."

The manager complies. "Don't kill me. Please. My fans at the little venue where I perform. They'll be heartbroken."

"If you do the ancient pick-a-number-between-one-and-ten routine with them, guessing they're already heartbroken." Tommy kicks open the door, the bright daylight rushing into the dim hallway.

He brings the manager into the parking lot, intrigued-looking customers huddled in clusters, an early-twenties guy with a backwards cap videoing the encounter.

Kurt's eyes widen through the pickup's windshield. Tommy opens a backdoor, pushes the manager inside, climbs in next to him. "Drive." He slams the door.

"Where?" Kurt asks.

"Anywhere but here. Go."

# TWENTY

The pickup is parked in an alley behind a vacant, gutted warehouse in an industrial neighborhood about five miles from Rose Lounge, a faded soup-company sign on the facade, a 1990s design to it. A wall of hedges shields the vehicle from highway view, the whoosh of traffic beyond it. Kurt sits in the driver's seat staring at the truck's ceiling, the bar manager fidgeting beside Tommy in back.

"Cops got to have my truck info by now," Kurt says. "Make . . . model . . . probably plates. We in it. They gonna find us. I feel it. Right in my bones."

"We're okay back here," Tommy says. "A passing cop car doesn't have an angle to us."

Kurt presses the heel of his hand against his eye. "Mama gonna lose her mind if I end up in jail." He jabs his index finger at Tommy. "I told you not to go in the dang bar."

"What was I supposed to do, not find out who tried to kill us?"

"Could've . . . done it a different way."

"What way?"

A pause. "I don't know," Kurt screams. "God."

The manager, a *Barry* nametag on his Hawaiian shirt, says, "Hey boys, how about some sleight of hand to lighten the mood?" He reaches into his pocket.

"Watch it," Tommy says, cocking the gun.

"Just my cards," Barry says, revealing a deck in his palm. "Always carry a set around." He fans them out. "Pick one."

"Pick a better way to avoid getting shot." Tommy smacks the deck out of his hands, hearts, spades, diamonds, and clubs flying through the cabin. "The man you called, is he tall, couple inches taller than me, and fit?"

"Yes. But I don't know the guy."

"You had his number and a reason to call him. Sounds like you know him pretty damn well."

"Umm . . . he's a customer. So I've seen him. But I don't know him, know him . . . you know?"

"No. You get the phone numbers of all your customers?"

"I . . . I never asked for his. He was the one who called me. Earlier in the week. Told me he was the guy who comes in and dances."

"Is that code for something?"

"No. Actual dancing. It's a little weird, but hey, power to him. He came into the bar three, maybe four times before. Always alone. Had a couple drinks, then went on the dancefloor for like an hour. Never interacts with anyone else when he's out there. Just dances by himself. I never even spoke to him in person."

"If you never spoke to him in person and don't even know his name, why the hell did he call you? What did he want from you?"

Barry nods at Kurt. "His sister. She must've given him my number. Alexa, what an interesting girl. Beautiful girl too. Whole staff loved her. Sad when she left us."

"So Alexa gave him your number. Why?"

Barry takes a deep breath. "Look, I didn't do anything illegal. Whatever this whole thing is, I just got caught up in the middle of it, okay?"

"I don't give a shit either way. We're not cops. The fact that we're running from them should be proof of that. We just want the truth. Without it, Alexa could be on the other end of a gun next."

Barry runs his fingers over the purplish lump on his forehead, winces. "You going to let me go if I tell you the story?"

"Yes."

"You got a cigarette? Let me get a smoke, huh?"

Kurt opens the glovebox, hands him a cigarette. "Don't have a lighter in here. Sorry."

The unlit Marlboro hangs from Barry's mouth. "So a few days ago, this FBI agent came into the bar. And—"

"Female, black hair, twenty-seven?"

"How'd you know that?"

"Don't worry about it. What did she ask you?"

"Same thing as you guys. Wanted to know where to find Alexa."

"Did you tell her?"

Barry looks at Kurt. "Your sister, she and I . . . even though I was her boss, I considered her a friend. She even came to one of my shows. Told me if the magic industry wasn't so corporatized, I'd be the next big thing. Which is exactly what I've been saying since—"

"Focus," Tommy says. "What did you tell the FBI agent about Alexa?"

"What I thought of her as a person. But she didn't seem to share my sentiment. Wouldn't admit what she needed her for, but I . . . had a feeling . . . it wasn't something good." A sigh. "But no way a sweet kid like her was involved in anything criminal. Right?"

"So you withheld information from the FBI?"

"I had no information to give. Never documented an address for Alexa when she started work. She was sort of drifting when she got to town. Think she lived out of her car for a couple nights. I heard also some motel. Unsure which."

"Then the FBI agent left?"

"And I immediately called Alexa to tell her the feds were looking for her. Number was disconnected. So I tried email. She replied. Said it was probably a misunderstanding. I asked how she was doing in general. Said great. New job. New townhouse."

"Where's this townhouse?"

"Don't know. Didn't ask."

Tommy rubs his brow. "None of this explains why one of your whack-job customers put on a ski mask and shot at us."

"He called me up a day after I emailed with Alexa. Said he was going to take care of this whole FBI misunderstanding for her. I thought . . . well terrific."

"He say how?"

"No. Just asked me for two favors. First, he wanted the name and number of the FBI girl who came into the bar, which I got from the card she left me. Second, he said if anyone else showed up asking questions about Alexa, to call him." He glances at Kurt. "Which is exactly what I did today when you came in. He said he was happy to help you out. Then gave me that Henderson address. I had no idea he'd be there with a rifle. He just . . . didn't seem the type. And why kill you? It doesn't make any sense."

"When was the last time this guy came into the bar?" Tommy asks.

"I guess it was the day he met Alexa. She was his server. They seemed to . . . hit it off. That was her second-to-last day working with us. That's my story. I've got nothing else."

Tommy lets out a long breath, runs his hand through his hair.

"Can I go now?" Barry asks.

"Almost. Here's what you're going to do. Call Rose Lounge, ask to speak to whoever's in charge while you're . . . out. Tell them you have a gambling problem. That—"

"I don't have a gambling problem."

"Jesus, I know Barry. It's just a cover. Tell them the man who snatched you was a debt collector. Say you're safe. But you need some surveillance footage to show the debt collector to prove you handed an envelope of money to his associate. The date happened to be Alexa's second-to-last day of work."

# TWENTY-ONE

Alexa Thoss provokes stares strutting through the Bellagio in yoga pants and a V-neck tee shirt. Bottled lust in the eyes of men, bottled envy the eyes of women. The headphones in her ears blast "Flowers in My Hair, Demons in My Head" by The Mystery Lights.

Polished marble floors glisten under her Converse sneakers, ornate chandeliers above her, as she makes her way into the casino.

She slips the headphones out, orders a strawberry daquiri at a bar. Then sucks a sip from the straw and adjusts her necklace, its black-stone charm resting atop her C-cup cleavage.

Eight men huddled at a nearby craps table. Three at the head in expensive blazers. She finishes her daquiri, orders a second, then strides toward the table.

The male eyes notice her. Some flick to a part of

her, face, tits, legs, then flick away. Others stare. She sidles her thin, five-four body to the table head, beside a man wearing a wedding ring and Rolex that must cost at least twenty grand.

"ID, miss?" a pit boss asks with a smile.

She passes him her driver's license. While he checks it, she swirls her straw in her icy red drink. She can feel the man beside her looking at her. He's about forty-five, thinning hair, halfway to handsome. He fidgets with his chips, as if a bit anxious thinking up an opening line.

"Good luck, miss," the pit boss says, handing her back the license.

She smiles. Then opens her purse, removes a green twenty-five-dollar chip, and places it on the pass line. A player at the other end of the table rolls the dice.

"Six, easy six," the croupier announces.

The man beside Alexa places more chips on the table, then says to her in a slight Southern accent, "Don't mean to intrude, but you should play the odds on that six. Back it up."

She sticks her straw in her mouth. Looks up at him. Sips. "I'm fine."

"All right, all right. Suit yourself. You . . . uh . . . here alone?"

She nods.

"From town or on vacation?" he asks.

"Neither."

"Yo eleven," the croupier announces as the next dice roll settles.

The married man leans down so his eyeline is level with Alexa's. "I'm here for a convention. Wealth management. You familiar with the business?"

"No."

"It's a wild ride. Lot of work. But very fulfilling."

"Eight, hard eight," the croupier announces.

"What sort of work do you do?" the married man asks her. "Or . . . you seem a little young. Are you still in school? Do you go to UNLV?"

"I do a little bit of this. A little bit of that."

"Cool. All right. Very cool." His complexion is a dash red.

The roller throws the dice. Two threes.

"Winner, six, hard six, winner," the croupier announces.

The married man pumps his fist. His buddy slaps his back. Another high-fives him. He rakes in his plentiful winnings.

"Maybe I was wrong," she says to him. "Should've played the odds like you."

"Eh, no regrets. That's my motto."

"What're you going to do with all that money, mister?"

"Try to turn it into more money." He has a sip of his Heineken. "That's what wealth managers do. Good ones at least. Turn money into more."

She sucks down the last of her daquiri. "The twenty-five dollars I won should be enough to buy myself another drink. Join me if you'd like." She picks up her two green chips and struts away from the table toward the bar. Behind her, she hears the man conversing with his two friends.

In a few seconds, he blurts, "Sure."

She doesn't stop walking, doesn't look back.

He trots to her side, says, "After a big win at the craps table, a self-respecting Savannah gentleman wouldn't allow a new friend to buy her own drink." He nods at a swanky lounge in the distance. "Want to try there?"

"Never been."

"I went last night. Think you'd like it."

"You don't know anything about me. How would you know I'd like it?"

He hesitates. "It's . . . uh . . . it's nice. The sort of place people generally . . . it's nice."

"Do wealth managers go to nice places often?"

"Of course. Wine and dine. Key element of the business."

"So if I gave you money, you could turn it into more?"

"Think of me like your personal ATM machine. Except your balance doesn't go down when I give you cash."

"Wow. Got a business card?"

He slips her one. "You have savings you're looking to invest? An inheritance from a deceased relative, perhaps?"

She eyes the card. It supplies what she needs, full name, email address, phone number. "My situation is . . . complicated."

"All shapes and sizes, young lady. All shapes and sizes." A chandelier brings out the sheen of sweat on his forehead.

They enter the bar, the lighting dimmer than the casino's. They share a table in back, sitting on the same side of a booth. An unseen pianist plays a tune.

She orders another daquiri, he a Johnnie Walker Blue. They have two more rounds while he explains how a big portion of his business involves selling his clients simple investments with complicated-sounding names at high fees. She pretends to be impressed.

"You're so interesting to talk to," she says. "The guys my age are immature."

"It's a fact of science, females mature quicker than men. That's why girls should always date older guys."

"I've never dated an older guy. My friends tell me all the time I should."

An awkward chuckle from him.

"Is your wife younger than you?" she asks.

"Eh . . . yes, but not like you. Three years. She's forty-three."

"Did she attend this convention with you?"

"No. No, she did not." He sips the booze in his glass, gazes down at it, watches the ice cubes drift. "Twenty-three years I've been married to her."

"Longer than I've been alive."

He laughs. Then seriousness consumes his face. "She's kind. And funny. And a great mother. But . . . I don't know."

"What? You can tell me."

"It's silly. You're going to think I'm silly."

"Nah ah."

He finishes his drink. "The feeling . . . the feeling I got when you looked at me for the first time at the craps table was . . . I never got that feeling once around her. Not when she first looked at me. Not during the two years we dated. Not during the twenty-three we've been married." He peers into his empty glass. "How's that for silly?"

She nods in an understanding way. Puts her hand on his knee. "I completely get it. Don't feel bad. I'm sure a lot of men are in the same position as you. What you can't do is be a slave to it. We only have one life. You know?"

"I know. God. I know all too well."

She pretends to check the time on her phone. "I've unfortunately got to get running. But later tonight, let's hang out again. You have a room in the hotel?"

"Suite. Amazing view of the Strip."

"Maybe you can show me. We can pop a bottle of

champagne. Celebrate your choice not to be a slave anymore." She rubs his thigh. "No regrets. What do you say?"

He looks into her eyes, a grapple between lust and decency in his. "I say yes."

She hugs him. "The cell number on your card, I'll text you later."

"Can't wait."

She stands, smiles at him over her shoulder, then leaves the bar. Walks the Bellagio until out of his sight, then clicks a tiny button on the bottom of her necklace charm, sending to her phone, via the app Cloud Drop, the recording the mini video camera hidden inside just made.

She calls her boyfriend. He answers and she says, "Hey babe. Just got a new one. Probably brings in half a mill a year. Once you hit him with your negotiating magic, sure it'll be a big payday for us."

"Good, love," he says, lacking his typical enthusiasm for a successful job.

"You okay? The last few days you've seemed a little preoccupied."

A pause. "We should . . . there is something . . . I need to tell you something."

# TWENTY-TWO

From his pickup, Kurt's eyes gravitate to a bill-board for the Electric Cheetah strip club above the highway bordering the abandoned soup warehouse. On it a blonde and brunette in cheetah-print bikinis on all fours, *OPEN 24/7* under them. In the rearview mirror, Tommy notices him staring. Kurt snaps his gaze away.

"Still nothing from your assistant manager," Tommy says, Barry's phone in his pocket.

Barry collects his playing cards from the truck's floor and crevices. "Give him a few minutes."

"It's been a few minutes."

"He's pretty busy. In case you forgot, a key employee was recently removed from the floor."

Tommy nods as if agreeing with the point. "How's your head?"

"Hurts still. You're lucky you have Alexa's safety in mind. If not, I'd take a swing at you for that."

"When this is all said and done, Barry, I'll buy you a lighter for that cigarette."

Silence for a while besides the rustle of cards. Then a ding from Tommy's pocket. He checks Barry's phone. A new email, subject line *Surveillance footage 2/23.*

"Let's see what we got," Tommy says.

Kurt and Barry lean toward him. Two files attached to the email, one named *Interior*, the second *Exterior*. Tommy opens the first, a grid of recordings from the four cameras inside Rose Lounge.

"Alexa's partner in crime," Tommy says, "about what time did he come in the day he met her?"

"He'd always stop by at night," Barry says. "Never too late when the dancefloor was packed. I remember he liked space to move out there. Probably . . . seven-ish."

Tommy fast-forwards to the timestamp just before seven PM. "Tell me when you see the asshole." He reduces the fast-forward speed, slow enough to make out faces.

"There I am," Barry says, excitement in his voice. He points at himself behind the bar mixing a drink.

"You've got presence back there. Look at that posture."

They watch the video a while longer. A man with shaggy hair enters Rose Lounge, his hands buried in the front pockets of his jeans.

"That's him," Barry blurts.

Tommy pauses the video. Zooms in on the guy. Mid-thirties, weathered good looks, casual designer clothing. Tall, broad, and lean, like an Olympic swimmer.

He saunters to the dancefloor, nobody else on it but an older couple, closes his eyes, and sways. He dances for a while. Then stops when he notices Alexa walk by with a drink tray.

He doesn't approach her. Instead sits at a high-top table in her section. His foot taps the base of his stool.

She comes over. He says something, no sound on the recording. They talk. He keeps tapping his foot. He emanates a nervous energy, yet seems to hold her attention. She appears guarded at first, turned half-way to him, her eyes checking her other tables. Then she faces him head on.

In a couple minutes, he takes out his phone. Types as she speaks as if saving her number. He has one drink, waves goodbye to her, and leaves.

Tommy notes the timestamp, 7:57 PM, then opens the second email attachment, *Exterior*, and fast-forwards to 7:57 PM on the surveillance footage of the parking lot. The man exits the bar, mounts a Ducati motorcycle.

Tommy pauses the video, zooms in on the bike's license plate. "Gotcha, dickhead."

"That's what I'm talking 'bout," Kurt says.

Tommy logs into a personal-records portal he has an account on for his former job at Canven Investigative Solutions, and inputs the motorcycle's plate number.

A DMV listing comes up for a six-foot-three thirty-seven-year-old named Dennis Notch, current address in Vegas. No other vehicles registered to his name. He must've been smart enough to purchase that gray van off the books.

Reading more of Dennis's info, Tommy says, "Originally from Maryland. Place called Poolesville. Parents still together. One brother. Dad's a pediatric surgeon."

He finds an education history. "Yale undergrad. Georgetown law. Top of his class." Next an employment breakdown. "Clerked for a future Attorney General. Then made junior partner at a corporate firm in DC." Toward the bottom of the page, Tommy notices a penal listing. "Huh. And spent time in the clink. Four years. Manslaughter."

"Bizarre," Barry says. He glances at an archived photo of suit-and-tie-wearing Dennis as a lawyer, about twenty-eight in it, hair short, expression prim and professional. "Looks like a Brooks Brothers ad. How do you go from that to . . . a guy in a ski mask who shoots people at horse farms?"

"That's between him and God," Kurt says. "All I care 'bout is getting my baby sister far away from this kook." He turns to Tommy. "So what's the plan?"

*Thudunt*. A booming noise overhead.

They look up at a helicopter, *Las Vegas Metro Police Department* painted on the side, an officer in SWAT gear hanging out pointing a rifle at them.

# TWENTY-THREE

A male voice blares from a police-helicopter speaker, "Thomas Dapino, step out of the truck, hands on the back of your head, knees on the ground."

"Oh shit, oh shit," Kurt says, his eyes jumping in the mirror between the chopper and Tommy. "I fucking told you I felt this in my bones and you—"

"Let's just . . . we need to stay calm."

"I'm up for aiding and abetting a fugitive. I ain't staying—"

"Good luck guys," Barry says. He opens the door, steps out of the truck in a surrender pose.

The sound of the blades booms through the open doorway. Kurt, raising his voice, says, "Let's try to ditch 'em in the truck."

"In a chopper they can track us. We'll eventually run out of gas and that'll be it."

"Then what you sayin', we just give up, turn ourselves in?"

Tommy peeks outside. "No, we're not giving up. Follow me." He sticks the gun in the waist of his jeans.

"Follow you where?"

Tommy hops onto the pavement. Sprints toward the street. Kurt stumbles out behind him. He drops his phone. It slides under the truck.

"Just leave it," Tommy says.

Kurt does, hustling beside him. "Where the hell you going?"

"We need to break the visual from the helicopter. Got to get inside somewhere."

Around them nothing but industrial buildings. Employee badges may be needed for access. But in the distance is a hotel-casino, a *Lucky Larry's* sign in front, the logo a leprechaun with a lecherous grin, a pot of gold at his feet.

"There," Tommy says, pointing at it. He bolts toward it, Kurt keeping pace. A mailman dropping off a package at a business gapes at the two guys whizzing toward him with a police helicopter above.

"Unpaid parking tickets," Tommy says as they pass.

"Stop where you are," the voice from the sky shouts.

Tommy can't hear himself breath above the roar of the chopper, but feels his lungs laboring. He and Kurt have covered almost a mile of ground, the side of the casino a few feet ahead.

Another loud noise cuts into the atmosphere. A siren. Tommy looks toward it, a police car zooming at them at about eighty miles per hour.

"When we turn the corner to go into the casino, no more running," Tommy says. "We can't let them know all this is for us." His footfalls soften. So do Kurt's. "There you go. Brisk walk, like a grandma in the park."

They make the turn with nonchalant expressions. And pass a couple uniformed valet attendants staring up at the chopper. Tommy and Kurt enter the casino through a revolving door.

The blasted air conditioning chills the sweat on Tommy's overheated body, an uncomfortable hot-cold sensation coursing through him.

Low ceilings, drab green carpet, a painting of Lucky Larry behind the front desk, each of his arms around a girl, his head up to their breasts, their hands cupping gold coins.

Tommy turns right, mixing into the crowd. He and Kurt pass a packed buffet. The average weight of a Lucky Larry's patron seems to be a solid fifteen percent above the American average, plenty atop motorized scooters.

The slot machines blink and ring. Tommy hasn't been inside a casino since a trip to Atlantic City nine years ago with his sister and some friends from the neighborhood in Queens. He remembers telling her the gambling machines were like big children's toys. She disagreed, informing him that underneath the playful noises and flashes is the unflinching determinism of statistical theory, computers inside programmed with precise payout goals. In the long run, the casino wins and the gambler loses.

Tommy slips into a giftshop.

"You kidding me?" Kurt whispers. "Now's the time to buy a collectible snow globe?"

Tommy grabs a baseball cap and tee shirt with the Lucky Larry's logo on them. He pays fifty-six bucks, exits with a plastic bag, progresses along the busy corridor.

On a mirrored wall, he sees two cops about a hundred fifty feet behind them scanning the crowd.

Kurt seems to spot them too. "We can only hide out in here for so long."

"I know."

"That dang chopper gonna be watching every damn exit for us."

"I know."

The hallway meets two others at an intersection, a lit sign directing toward various places on the premises.

"I'm making the next left," Tommy says. "Follow my lead." They turn. Two more patrolling cops at the end of this hall, heads swiveling.

Tommy ducks inside a men's room, Kurt tailing. Tommy rips off his tiger-print shirt and Yankees cap, chucks them in an empty stall, then slips on his new Lucky Larry's gear. He flips on a sink, washes the dry blood off his forearm, the man beside him avoiding eye contact. Tommy waits for the guy, the only other in here, to leave, and catches the door slab just before it closes.

He peers out the crack. Notices a nearby cop. As soon as the officer turns his back to the bathroom, Tommy head-signals to the hallway, and he and Kurt step out.

Tommy picks up his pace to faster than before, yet not quite fast enough to draw attention. He turns at a sign directing toward *Visitor Parking*. In a bit they enter a five-story parking structure. A couple dozen patrons bustle from cars to the casino and vice versa.

"Fewer people on the upper levels," Tommy says. "Fewer witnesses."

"Jesus, witnesses for what? What're you about to do?"

Tommy leads him up the staircase to the fourth story, the highest without overhead exposure to the circling chopper. Tommy leans against a concrete beam, pretends to read a message on his phone. Kurt paces, bites his knuckle, mutters under his breath.

A group of three comes up to their level, walks to an SUV. Tommy scopes them. They seem too put-together for what he has in mind. His eyes return to his phone.

A few minutes later a lone man steps onto the level. A slight redness to his cheeks, half his shirt untucked. Drunk. Perfect.

Tommy walks to him. "Hello sir, my name is Garret. I work with the resort."

The man stops, eyeballs him. In his Lucky Larry's shirt and hat, Tommy looks like one of the valet attendants out front.

"Congratulations," the man says. "I probably just paid half your salary at the roulette wheel." He continues to his car.

Tommy trails him. "We appreciate your patronage, sir. Which is why we'd like to extend you a courtesy service."

"A comp?"

"Yes. Totally free."

"I don't have a lot of time. What? Quick, go."

"We know our guests often enjoy our cocktails at the gaming tables. To help them avoid pricey DUIs, Lucky Larry's has started to employ courtesy drivers. It'd be my pleasure to take your car home for you. We'll gladly pay for your transportation in a taxi."

The man folds his arms. Hiccups. "Thanks, but I can drive home."

Tommy notices a mustard stain on the guy's sleeve. "As an encouragement for this safe-driving program, Lucky Larry's is offering a week's worth of buffet tickets for all participants."

The man's eyes widen. "Crab legs included or I still got to pay extra for those?"

"These are platinum tickets, sir. If you want to bring in a deep sea fishing net and haul a bunch of crab legs out for later, we can't legally stop you."

The man's brow furrows. He hiccups again. "What I got to do?"

"Just give me your keys. I'll pull your car around front, wait for you. Go to the valets by the entrance, tell them you're participating in the courtesy-driver program. They'll hail you a free cab, plus break you off those buffet tickets. I'll follow your taxi home in your car."

Another hiccup. "Screw it. Sure." He tosses Tommy his keys, points at a black Toyota Camry, and heads toward the staircase.

Tommy climbs in the car, pulls up to Kurt. With an impressed expression, he gets in. Tommy descends to ground level, exits the parking structure in a vehicle no cops are looking for yet. And drives away from the casino.

# TWENTY-FOUR

Dennis Notch, holding a colorful bouquet of flowers, waits in line at a florist shop a few blocks off the Strip. The white-haired woman in front of him, who told the cashier she's paying via check, searches through her big purse with a slow, arthritic hand. Dennis's foot taps.

"Oh, I think I have it," the woman says. "Shucks, no, that's not my checkbook. A birthday card from my grandson I can't bring myself to throw out. Such a nice message inside."

"Jesus Christ, lady," Dennis blurts. "My hair is going to be the same color as yours by the time I get out of here."

The woman and cashier peer at him. Neither replies.

"Have some respect, huh?" a man in line behind

115

him says.

Six-foot-three Dennis glares at the short man. Five seconds pass. The man gulps, looks away.

In a couple minutes, the old woman pays by check, then Dennis by credit card. He steps outside, cracks his knuckles, then neck. The accumulating stress from the last few days has weighed on him. Before he sees Alexa for the conversation he's been avoiding, he could use a chemical aid.

He turns behind the florist shop, fishes a small nitrous oxide canister from his pocket, and snorts it. A euphoric lightheadedness puts his problems into perspective. He tucks his tank top into his designer jeans, stuffs the flowers in the front, and starts his Ducati bike.

He motors toward a residential part of Vegas, his long, dark hair dancing in the wind, the purples and pinks of the flower petals flapping against the spider-web tattoo on his chest he got in prison.

Soon he pulls into Emerald Heights, a townhouse development where he purchased a unit last month.

The home's purpose is twofold. Applying his extensive legal knowledge, he bought it through an anonymous shell corporation he set up, a tool for laundering the profits from the scams he runs with his girlfriend Alexa, cloaking a chunk of the money as real estate rental income. Also, she lives there rent-free, an upgrade from the shitty motel she called home after arriving in Vegas.

He parks his motorcycle, takes a deep breath, knocks on her door.

She opens it. And jumps on him, her spandex-wrapped legs circling his waist, her arms around his shoulders. He drops the flowers, his hands going to her ass. They make out crossing the doorway into the foyer. He presses her back to the wall.

"Hi," she says. And smiles.

"Hi babe."

"You shoulda seen me at the Bellagio before. I was like a ninja on this guy. Hi-yah." She kisses Dennis's cheek, then sucks the bottom of his ear. "Let's go upstairs."

"Definitely." He sets her down. "But we need to talk about that thing first. I want to get it out of the way."

She collects the flowers from the stoop and closes the door. "Did you bring me these to apologize about something?"

"No. I . . . I brought you them because . . . you are you."

She smells them. "I've never been to the beach. But I imagine this is what the beach is like."

"Do you have a brother?"

Her smiles fades. "Yes. Why?"

"Do you have a photo?"

"Umm. Sure." She walks into the kitchen, plops the flowers on the table, picks up her phone. Her thumbs tap the screen. She shows Dennis a picture of the blond kid who accompanied Dapino to the horse farm.

Dennis lets out a long exhale. "How come you never told me you had a brother?"

"Never came up. Why do—"

"A lot of important things do not come up. So you bring them up."

"This wasn't important. My mom tried her Jesus-freak shit on both of us. Worked on him, not me. Me and Kurt . . . don't have a lot in common. We fell out of touch. You ran into him?"

"I . . . Alexa, I thought you were in danger. I was just trying to help."

"In danger from my brother?"

"The guy he was with."

"What guy?"

Dennis grabs a bottle of Stoli vodka from the top of her fridge, pours some in a Solo cup, passes it to her.

"I'm okay," she says.

"Well . . . you might not be."

A bend of confusion to her face.

"I encouraged you to take part in this . . . not technically legal . . . business venture with me," he says. "Thus, it is my responsibility to keep you safe from its risks."

"What risks? What're you talking about, Den?"

"That FBI agent who was asking questions about you at Rose Lounge."

"I thought you resolved that."

"I . . . massaged the truth into a slightly different form."

She paces. "So you lied?"

"That is too harsh a word."

"Stop talking like a lawyer."

"I am a lawyer. Well, disbarred. Still am at heart I suppose."

"You said you could talk to the FBI agent like a real lawyer would and handle this. Give her . . . what did you call it, reasonable doubt? That I didn't scam anyone."

"I tried. Really. But she did not seem to believe me. She was building a case against you, said she had a victim willing to testify in court."

"This is bad, Dennis. This is really bad. And you didn't think to tell me?"

"Unfortunately, babe, it gets worse."

A burst of laughter from her.

He chugs the shot of Stoli. "I will keep us out of prison. But I am warning you . . . I had to take some extreme measures. How about you sit down?"

"I'm all right."

He rubs the five o'clock shadow on his chin. "The FBI agent." A moment. "I sort of . . . kidnapped her."

Alexa stops pacing. Stares into his eyes. "You . . . what?"

"Only to protect you. Both of us. My goal—"

"Are you being serious right now?" She scrutinizes his face as if for a flash of sarcasm. He shows none. She grasps the Stoli bottle, swigs from the spout. "How could this accomplish anything other than getting us in much more trouble than we're already in?"

"If I could make this fed fear for her life, scare her into telling me the witness's name, I could do the same to him, discourage him from testifying. The case against you crumbles."

"Where is she now?"

"Secure in my house."

"Oh man. You think she is going to just walk away after giving up the witness? She's going to bring the wrath of hell down on you for kidnapping her."

"That is something I will see to."

"Milking wannabe cheats for a few bucks I was fine with. I didn't sign up for a kidnap plot." A pause. "And my brother? He got caught up in this disaster too? How?"

He pulls up a news article on his phone titled "Suspect in Kidnap of FBI Agent Breaks Out of Jail." He hands it to her.

She reads for a while. "Why do they think her boyfriend took her instead of you?"

"That I do not know. What I do know is this Dapino fellow is not only out of jail, but in Vegas. With your brother. And he is looking for you."

"Me?"

"Likely so you could lead him to me. And if he exposes what I did to his girlfriend, I am fucked."

"No. We are fucked." She grips her hips, closes her eyes, and dips her head toward her shoulder. "And he's coercing Kurt to get to us?"

"No coercion from what I saw. They seem to be working together. Like a duo."

"This is getting real batty."

"I assumed the guy Dapino was with was just some goon, that he made up the line about being your brother."

She scrolls through her phone, pulls up the contact *Kurt*, and dials. A few moments. She hangs up. "No answer. Ugh. Where is he now?"

"I have not seen either of them since I . . . confronted them."

"Physically?"

"You could say that."

"Is Kurt okay?"

"They got away. He is fine."

"None of this is fine, Den." She slaps the wall.

"I will make it fine."

"How? You're in possession of an abducted FBI agent. I can imagine all the people looking for her. Someone will find her eventually."

"I realize. I am getting rid of her today. Kreshnik and I will bury any evidence of the kidnap in the desert."

"There's evidence you took her?"

"Well, of course." A moment. "Her."

A moment. "No. You can't. Just—"

"At this point, I can't simply let her loose. You said it yourself."

"Yes. But there must be some other . . . I . . . uh . . . oh, Den."

"If she goes free, you and I both land in prison. And stay for a long time. That is not the future I envision for us."

She runs her fingers down his cheek. "You can't kill some innocent girl to change our future. You're super smart. Find an alternative."

He holds his gaze on her for a while. "If that is what you wish, then ... that is what you shall get. I will brainstorm."

"And what about this problem with her boyfriend and my brother?"

He clenches his teeth. "Honey ... one thing at a time. Please. I will ... keep you posted." He downs another vodka shot and leaves.

# TWENTY-FIVE

Tommy and Kurt cruise through Las Vegas in the drunk gambler's Camry. Soon the cops will connect the stolen vehicle to Tommy and direct the chopper to search for it.

"The police are definitely looking for you too," Tommy says. "But you can walk away from this unscathed. Just tell them I forced you to go along with me. I won't be offended."

Kurt squints in the sun shining through the windshield. "But if I tell them you forced me, ain't you going to be in more hot shit than you already are?"

"Yes."

"And don't you need my help when we roll up on Dennis?"

"It would be appreciated. But he's a dangerous guy. Rolling up on him could get messy. Which is why I want to give you an out now."

A pause. "Nah. I won't do you dirty like that."
He dabs some sweat on his chin with his tee shirt.
"Besides, I came out here to make sure Alexa is okay.
And didn't do it yet. Ain't quittin' now."

Tommy pats his shoulder. Soon he pulls into
the parking lot of a Home Depot with various simi-
lar-looking cars and tucks the Camry among them.

He and Kurt exit. Tommy lowers his Lucky Larry's
cap, concealing his face from customers, and paces to a
sandy expanse bordering the road. Dust kicks up from
under their feet as they tread toward Dennis Notch's
address, Google Maps routing them on Tommy's
phone.

A text message comes in from Josh: *U still alive?*
Tommy writes back: *Not only alive getting close.*
Josh: *Be careful.*
Tommy: *If I don't you gonna tell my mom on me?*
Josh: *I don't know what that's supposed to mean.
Anyway guess what?*
Tommy: *??*
Josh: *That girl Michelle I told you about. We're
going out again. Tonight. She's really cool. She has this
job where she works on robots that clean garbage out
of the ocean so dolphins and stuff don't get messed up
by it. Since I'm also in tech she can talk to me about it
and I understand her. And when I tell her about the
SQL queries I write at work she gets it too. It's good.*
Tommy: *Nice.*
Josh: *Also she likes my jokes. Also she's pretty.*
"Dammit," Tommy says, a sharp pain in his calf.
"What?" Kurt asks.

Tommy looks down. A cactus by his leg. A needle
must've poked him.

Kurt chuckles. "Not much experience stepping

around those in New York?"

"Not much experience with sun like this either."
The heat burns the back of his neck. "Must really whet
a cannibal's appetite."

"Rather that than revving up some . . . some, like,
Eskimo . . . some Eskimo's appetite."

"What the hell does that mean?"

"I'd take the Nevada heat over the cold in New
York any day. Was trying to make a joke about it, but it
. . . got away from me."

"That thing went nowhere fast."

"All right. I admitted it."

"Anyway, I'm a San Diego guy now. No more cold."

"Ah . . . but you got that Queens vibe. You still
gonna be Queens, no matter where you live." A
moment. "I kinda like it. Don't lose it out in California."

They don't speak for about a quarter mile. Then
Kurt asks, "So what's our move when we get there?"

Tommy waits for a passing car to distance from
them, grips the pistol cloaked beneath his shirt, and
hands it to Kurt. "First off, better you hold onto this
than me. If we get busted by the cops, and they find a
gun on me registered to someone else, the hot shit you
spoke of will reach a boil."

"Sorry. 'Bout before. Freezing up with this at that
Rose place, making you have to go up in there with it."

"Don't worry about it. Things could get a little
tense at Dennis's. You might have to point that to
scare him. You've got to give the impression you've
fired it before. Think you can handle that, cowboy?"

Kurt secures the pistol in the back of his jeans. He
takes a deep breath.

# TWENTY-SIX

Dennis roots through a box in his garage for a nitrous oxide canister. He finds one and snorts it. He kicks his head back, the high tingling his face.

"Fuck me," he says toward the ceiling. "Fuck me."

Gentle, young Alexa. She doesn't know what's good for her. But Dennis does. He will shield his beautiful girlfriend from the world's ugly side, which exposed itself to him in prison.

On his first day of lockup, a few Black inmates called him Denise instead of Dennis. His problems worsened from there. After a few months, his aggressors were on the verge of killing him.

He needed protection, so, as a White boy, struck a deal with the skinheads. They made him shank one of their enemies, a rat, in the shower. Though he hesitated at first, Dennis plunged a sharpened toothbrush handle into his jugular. He still recalls the way the blood swirled into the water on the shower's white tile floor. As compensation, the skinheads watched his back. They let him lift weights with them in the gym. Taught him how to fight.

Dennis does not like violence. But after his stint in prison, is aware it is often a necessary part of survival.

His phone vibrates. A text from his Albanian friend and business associate, Kreshnik.

The message: *On my way to your house. You have supplies I need for my disposal services?*

Dennis's reply: *Got it all. See you soon dude.*

He enters his den, the pool out back visible through the window, a few beer bottles on the edge he needs to clean up, empties from some drinking he did with his pool guy after his last shift.

Through the home-wide speaker system, Dennis streams Prince's "Raspberry Beret" and climbs the stairs. He passes an oil painting on the foyer wall of a woman with a smile so intense it has ripped her bottom lip, a dab of blood trickling out.

He dances to the music in the hallway. Then opens the door to the curtains-shut guest bedroom. Handcuffed to the bed is Jordana, a couple pounds lighter in her gala dress since he kidnapped her, a ball gag in her mouth, a black-and-blue oval under her left eye from his punch the other night.

Her gaze moves to him. He lifts his arms over his head, his long fingers almost touching the eight-foot ceiling, and picks up dancing to the music, his wrists rotating, hips swaying. He gyrates around the edges of the bed.

The song finishes. He sits on the mattress and undoes her gag. "You have held out long enough. I commend you, but cannot let this behavior continue. I am giving you one last chance to provide the name of the witness."

"I know how situations like this work. Whether I give you the name now, or gave it to you two days ago, you were going to kill me anyway."

"You are correct. The choice is around how you will be killed. If you do not give me the name, my associate and I will put you in the bathtub and slice you up piece by piece until you bleed to death." He lifts an index finger. "Or . . . you provide the name and your death becomes painless. A simple bullet to the back of the head."

She stares into his eyes. She seems to notice something in them. He struggles to conceal his discomfort.

"You're scared," she says.

"Of who? You?"

"No. Of what's next. You must know you won't get away with this."

"If the FBI was going to find me, they would have done so already." He pulls a knife from his jeans, engraved on one side of the blade *Ecstasy* and on the other *Misery*. "The witness's name, please."

"Go ahead and cut me. Nothing I can do about it. But let me assure you of this. My boyfriend will find you. Even after I'm long gone. And he will kill you."

He smirks. "Your idiot boyfriend somehow got himself accused of the kidnap. If I do not take him out, the police will."

"Are you being serious? He got pinned for this?"

Dennis snickers. "You are apparently the only person in law enforcement who knows the truth. And you are about to die. By coming after my Alexa, you not only signed your own death sentence, but ruined your boyfriend's life. You should have backed off when I called you as her lawyer. All of this could have been avoided. Shame."

She lets out a long exhale. "If Tommy got accused of anything, it was . . . a mistake. But you ruining Alexa's life, that was avoidable. That is nobody's fault but yours."

"Alexa is . . . she is fine, just fine."

"I've been to that trailer she grew up in. She comes from nothing. Assuming you gained her trust, bought her some things, reeled her into your sick little world. Then convinced her to go out to casinos and dangle her ass in front of married guys. What sort of a boyfriend monetizes his girlfriend's ass?"

"She was not born into a billion-dollar wine fortune like you. But nature did bless her with certain physical assets. I guided her into leveraging them to improve her earning power. I did her a favor."

"I was lucky being born into my family. But instead of being a typical trust fund brat, I tried to do something with my life." She nods at her wrist restraints. "Seems it didn't end up so great for me. But I at least tried. What's your excuse?"

"Excuse for what?"

"Oh come on. You're eloquent. Sound like people I went to Stanford with. And you have perfect teeth, indicative of orthodontic care at a young age. Meaning you were born into a good family too. Parents with resources who took care of your medical bills, paid for an education. I've met plenty of criminals during my time as an FBI agent. Rarely are they brought up like you. But you became a fuck-up just like them. A federal agent chained to your bed, threatening to cut me into pieces. Is there an excuse?"

He glances at the floor. "You put yourself into this situation, not me."

"I don't think you really believe that. I don't think

you're happy this is how your life turned out."

"Don't worry about me."

"I'm very worried about you. Alexa is an impressionable country girl, probably infatuated with your McMansion. But the longer she's in a big city, the more aware she'll become of other options out there. Better men than you. Guarantee you it's started. And her infatuation will wear off. I'm guessing the moment an agent at an interrogation table slides her a plea deal to give you up. If Tommy doesn't bring you down first, she will."

"She loves me. She would never betray me."

"We'll see."

The sound of the doorbell fills the house. "No, you will not see. My associate is here." Dennis stuffs the ball gag back in her mouth. "Your last sight will be my knife carving through your skin and bones."

# TWENTY-SEVEN

Tommy, who just rang Dennis's doorbell, sets a folded piece of paper in his driveway, situates a pebble on top to keep it in place, and hides behind a bush beside the home's entrance.

He stares at the door. It opens, 80s pop music flowing outside. Dennis surfaces with a baffled expression peering at a personless stoop.

His eyes locate the slip of paper about eight feet away. Tommy pulled it from a trashcan in front of a nearby home. Just a receipt for a pair of women's shoes. However, folded and arranged under a rock, it looks important. And, as expected, provokes Dennis's curiosity.

He walks outside, descends the stoop's two steps to the driveway, and approaches the shoe receipt. His back faces Tommy, who rushes out from behind the bush. Tommy wraps an arm around his throat, squeezes a hand over his mouth.

Dennis's long body thrashes, his oily hair in Tommy's eyes. "Hey scumbag," Tommy says. He steps toward the home's entrance. "Take me to Jordana."

Dennis yanks a knife from his pocket and jabs it backward. It rips Tommy's shirt, slices his hip.

"Ahh," Tommy mutters. Not a deep cut, but blood drawn, a warm stream on his flesh. Dennis breaks free. He clutches the knife blade down, like a prison shank. Like Tommy, he must've learned how to fight behind bars.

Dennis slashes at him. Tommy jumps to the right, crouches, and slugs him in the kidney. Dennis slashes again, Tommy bobbing left. He punches Dennis in the rib, rises, and hits him in the chin. Dennis rams his knee into Tommy's gut and lifts the knife in a stabbing position.

Tommy clasps his wrist before he impales him, and shouts, "Now."

Kurt pops out from behind a bush pointing his gun at Dennis. "Drop the blade or I put one in you."

Dennis, panting, takes in Kurt. He opens his hand, the knife falling, clinking on the pavement. But he does not appear defeated, wearing a cocky grin as if he knows something they don't.

"Get your ass inside," Tommy says, kicking the blade away.

"You are making a mistake."

"Am I at the wrong house? I'm looking for a scraggly schmuck who hits girls half his size. There're two of you on the block?"

In the distance, the sound of an engine. Tommy's gaze moves between a gap in the large palm trees on the lawn.

A black SUV glinting in the sun zips into view. And turns into the driveway. Through the windshield, the wide-bodied driver peers at the confrontation near the stoop. He jumps out of his car. Thick muscles under a tee shirt with a workout-supplement logo, a ring in each ear, one in his nose.

"Your back," Tommy yells to Kurt.

Kurt turns over his shoulder. While his head is still rotating, Dennis's friend's big fist bashes into it, sending it the other way. Kurt collapses, his gun springing from his grip upon asphalt impact.

The friend steps over unconscious Kurt toward Tommy, who clenches Dennis's tank top and backpedals up the two steps. In the foyer, Tommy kicks the door, hoping to close it on the friend.

The slab hurtles toward the doorframe. But a bulky arm stops it. The friend's angry head emerges inside. Dennis elbows Tommy in the wrist, trying to split his grip from the tank top. Tommy holds on. Dennis headbutts him. Tommy still holds on.

The friend slides a pistol from the waist of his form-fitting sweats. He points it at Tommy, who ducks. A gunshot booms, a hole in the wall.

"Jesus," Tommy says. He bear-hugs Dennis from behind and charges into the friend. The tangle of three bodies smacks into the wall. Amid the frenzy, Tommy slaps the gun.

It skips across the hardwood floor into the den, bangs into a wall, and bounces down a hallway. The friend chases after it. No way Tommy could beat him to it carrying Dennis. So lets him go. Dennis bolts toward the front door while Tommy does the same toward the weapon.

The friend, a step ahead of him, nears it. Tommy slides across the floorboards headfirst like a baseball player stealing home. His hand contacts it, but doesn't grasp it. The pistol zips farther down the hallway and hops into another room, a home gym.

Tommy scrambles inside. Behind him heavy stomping. The pistol beneath a rack of dumbbells. Tommy drops to his knees, stretches his arm under it.

Before he can grab the gun, a big sneaker pounds his back. His face whacks a weight.

Pain crawling up his cheekbone, he again reaches for the weapon. But the musclehead clasps his ankles, rips him backward. The smell of the hard-rubber flooring up Tommy's nose as his face rumbles against it. He spins onto his back, sees the guy looming over him with a forty-five-pound iron plate.

The musclehead hammers the plate down at him. Tommy rolls out of the way, just avoiding it, a clonk resounding, then kicks the guy in the side of the knee. He growls, his posture hitching.

Tommy pops him in the nose with a left jab. The cheek with a right hook. He attempts another right, but the guy blocks it, then backhands him. Tommy flails. He grabs a ten-pound kettlebell, swings it at his head.

The guy ducks, the momentum throwing Tommy off balance. He stumbles into an elliptical machine a few feet away. Then turns around and hurls the kettle-bell at the musclehead's stomach.

A grunt. A backpedal. The musclehead regains his composure, picks up a barbell, reaches back with it like a javelin.

Tommy clutches a sit-up bench as a shield. The end of the barbell bangs into it, the force knocking him into a cooler. He drops to the floor, the water jug too. Liquid cascades from it.

He tries to stand but slips on the wet surface. The

musclehead on his knees by the dumbbell rack. Grabbing for the gun.

Tommy gets his footing. Runs toward him. Loses it again. The musclehead has the firearm. Tommy winces, readying for a bullet.

"Don't," a voice says.

They look toward it.

Kurt.

Standing in the doorway with a bloody nose, his pistol fixed on the musclehead.

Who whips his gun off Tommy and onto Kurt. Then fires. Hits Kurt in the chest.

"No," Tommy screams.

A circle of blood on his shirt, Kurt staggers backward into the hallway. But keeps his shooting arm steady. He pulls the trigger.

Nails the musclehead an inch above his left eye.

His brawny body topples into the dumbbell rack, knocking off half a dozen weights. He collapses facedown. One more weight falls, hits his back. He's still.

Soaked Tommy springs to his feet, skids across the watery floor to Kurt, lying on his back. Tommy sticks his palm over the gunshot wound to control the bleeding. "I'm here, man."

Kurt glances down at the blood ringing Tommy's fingers. "I can't die."

"You won't."

Kurt's breaths are wispy. "I ain't never been with a girl."

"Don't think about—"

"What if I die and I ain't never been with a girl? Why God do that to me? Bad luck?"

"Don't talk."

Tommy pulls his phone from his jeans, dials 9-1-1. A dispatcher answers. "My buddy's been shot," Tommy says. "Nine six seven Hargave Street. Vegas."

He hangs up, returns his red hands over the wound. The 80s pop music still pulses through the house.

Almost ten minutes after the call, an ambulance siren. Tommy, containing the bleeding until help arrived, can focus on other objectives.

First, intel. He digs through the musclehead's sweatpants' pockets until finding a cellphone. He uses the corpse's thumbprint to unlock the screen, then disables locking so he can get back in later.

He darts through the hallway, opens a door, checks inside for a sign of Jordana. No. Another. No. The whole first floor, no.

Two paramedics burst through the open front entryway.

Tommy points toward Kurt.

They scurry that direction. Two cops file in behind them. One stares at Tommy. A flash of recognition in his expression.

"Freeze Dapino," he shouts, reaching for his gun.

Tommy runs upstairs. The two officers chase him.

"Jordana," Tommy yells. He opens a door. No. Another. No.

A metallic banging behind a third. He sprints toward it, the officers a couple paces behind. He discerns a squeaking noise too, bedsprings maybe.

He opens the door. A metal headboard slamming into the wall. A disheveled female chained to the bed.

He concentrates on the face, obscured with flapping dark hair and a gag. The nose, the defined cheekbones, the green eyes.

"Baby," he says.

Jordana stops tossing. A sigh of relief flows around the gag in her mouth.

He runs to her as the cops run inside.

They point pistols at him. But he ignores them, brushing the hair from Jordana's face. He undoes her gag, Kurt's blood on his fingers dotting her cheeks. They kiss.

"Agent Quick?" a cop says.

"Hello," she says.

A moment. "Did this man . . . didn't he kidnap you?"

She laughs. "No." Then looks Tommy up and down. "But he may've kidnapped a bellhop at a shitty casino."

# TWENTY-EIGHT

Tommy stands alone in a breakroom at the FBI's Las Vegas field office, gazing at the CPR instructions poster on the wall. He drinks lukewarm coffee from a paper cup, his clothes still damp from the spilt water jug in Dennis's gym.

A middle-aged man in a blue suit enters the small room. His hair, a razor shave around the sides with a curly patch on top, gives him the bearing of a Muppet Baby. "Thomas Dapino?"

"Who wants to know?"

"I'm Earnest Blosh. The FBI's Special Agent in Charge here. I heard you were done giving your official statement."

"You heard right."

"Well, this is a federal building. You can't just hang out if you don't have any additional business."

Tommy eyeballs his head. "Just finishing up my coffee. I don't plan to stick around for a haircut recommendation if that's what you're implying."

"Why would I be implying that?"

Tommy shrugs. Blosh scopes his reflection in the glass over the vending machine. Jordana steps inside.

"There she is," Tommy says.

She changed out of the red gala dress into a blue-and-gold FBI tee shirt, plus jeans and sneakers the bureau must've picked up for her at a nearby mall. Considering all she's been through the last three days, she looks terrific. She rubs his arm.

"Finish up that coffee, then please see yourself out," Blosh says to Tommy, then marches out of the room.

"What's up with him?" Jordana asks.

"If I looked like that, I'd be testy too. You guys should add his barber to your Ten Most Wanted list." Tommy checks the time on his phone. "I probably should be going soon. I want to swing by the hospital to see how Kurt is doing."

"From what I hear, he'll be okay."

"Thankfully. Too bad the damn kid didn't even get what he came out here for."

"Which was?"

"His sister. To make sure she was okay."

A moment. "He sounds like a great guy. Mystery how he could be related to that conniving bitch."

"I was at the same trailer you were. Guessing they didn't have the rosiest childhood. That can do a number on someone."

"I know plenty of people who had bad childhoods and didn't grow up to be honey-trapping blackmailers. Alexa Thoss is a professional manipulator. When we find Dennis, she's going down with him."

Jordana may be right about Alexa deserving retribution. Yet, Tommy is worried about her too, out there with that maniac Dennis. Before coming to Vegas, Tommy promised Kurt he'd help his sister. Even with Jordana safe, Tommy feels obligated to keep his promise. The least he can do after Kurt saved his life.

Jordana's phone rings. She answers a FaceTime call, her mom and dad on the screen at their house in Napa, a Picasso painting on the wall behind them.

"Hey guys," Jordana says.

"Sweetheart, are you at the office?" her dad asks.

"Of course."

"Oh no, no, go back to San Diego," her mom says. "After this ordeal? No work. Rest."

"No rest until we catch the guy."

"This is your fault," her dad tells her mom. "She gets her tenacity from you."

Jordana's mom rolls her eyes. Then says, "After you catch him, maybe you can finally apply that tenacity to something safe, like supplier negotiations at the family company. You can't keep putting yourself—"

"I'm an FBI agent, mom. I will be until I retire."

A sigh from her mom. "I had to try."

"I know."

"Come see us when your case is over. We'll send the plane. Bring Tommy. We can make another long weekend out of it."

Jordana angles her phone to include Tommy in the frame. He smiles, waves to her parents.

"Tommy," her dad says. "Sounds like you went through just as much hell as my daughter the last few days. Madness."

"Arresting you like that," her mom says, "I couldn't even sleep. Both of us."

"Jordana had it a lot worse than me," Tommy says.

"You raised a tough girl."

"We'll celebrate the end to all this in Napa," her dad says. "A party at the estate. All the aunts, uncles, and cousins. I'll arrange some live music. Tommy, what's your favorite band?"

"I trust your taste, Mister V."

"I'll make a few calls."

"I've got to get back at it," Jordana says. "Call you guys tomorrow."

Her parents wave. "Bye you two," her mom says.

Jordana hangs up.

"Good luck nabbing Dennis," Tommy says. "I'm going to check into a motel."

"Screw that. You pulled me out of that nutjob's lair today. You deserve a lot better than a motel. Get us a penthouse at the nicest place in Vegas. Mom and dad will pick up the tab."

The only way to guarantee Alexa's safety from Dennis is to put him in a cell or coffin. Though the FBI has the same goal, rules and regulations will slow them down. Lone operator Tommy could get to him faster.

Even if Jordana condoned his vigilante mission behind the FBI's back, her knowledge of it would jam her into an ethical predicament. He must keep his doings far from her. They can't share a hotel room. Besides, he feels weird accepting a handout from her parents.

"Appreciate the offer, hon," he says, "but I'm so wiped, I'm probably going to just pass out early. Don't want your mom and pops to blow money on some fancy hotel room if I'll just be looking at the pillows. I found this place online called the Bonanza Inn. Seems fine."

"Right. Okay." She leans against the vending

machine. "If I get a minute, let's try to squeeze in a quick dinner."

"Sounds good."

"Love you."

"Love you too." He kisses her and leaves, plotting in his mind a move on Dennis.

# TWENTY-NINE

Shower water from the Bonanza Inn crashes down on Tommy as he envisions Alexa's face. If she is dating Dennis, good chance she is unaware how dangerous he is.

Tommy lets his sore body soak for a while, despite the cuts on his forearm and hip, and his sunburnt neck, stinging in the stream.

He steps out and dries himself with the cheap motel's coarse towel, 777 stitched on one end, $$$ the other. With it around his waist, he wanders out of the bathroom. Yellow walls, noisy air conditioning, the Vegas Strip far off but visible through the shear curtain over the window.

His eyes gravitate to the night table. Beside his phone is that of the musclehead, whose name was Kreshnik, Tommy learned going through it. Stealing a dead accomplice's property was one of today's details Tommy didn't mention to the FBI when they interviewed him at the office.

He sits on the bed, leans against the headboard, above it the room's sole piece of art, a painting of a single-pump gas station along a road in the Nevada desert at dusk, a 1950s feel to it, a light on in a station window, no humans in sight.

Dennis has no reason to believe Kreshnik is dead. So from Kreshnik's phone, Tommy texts him: *Where are you man?*

Tommy flips on the TV. Waits for a response. Five minutes pass, nothing. Fifteen, still no. A half hour, nope. Dennis, now on the run, must've been smart enough to destroy the phone he's been using, fearing the feds may get the number and trace his signal.

Tommy needs another strategy.

While in Kreshnik's phone, he noticed a conversation today between him and contact *Alexa*. She has no reason to believe Kreshnik is dead either. Tommy pulls up their exchange.

Alexa: *Hey. Den said he might be doing a job with u today??*

Kreshnik: *I don't want to discuss this over phone.*

Alexa: *Chill. I'm not going to show the cops. He said he wouldn't go thru w it. But something about the way he said it I don't believe him. Try to talk him out of it if you could? There has to be another way to solve this.*

Kreshnik: *Do not contact me about this. And tell your boyfriend to learn how to keep his mouth shut around you.*

Tommy has something to work with here. He lacks a direct path to Dennis, but maybe can track down Alexa, use her to locate her boyfriend.

While he ponders an angle, his own phone

vibrates.

A text from Jordana: *Think I'll have time for dinner later. Where you want to go? Xoxo*

He can't see her tonight. Unsure how to reply, he ignores the message, telling himself he'll think of a good excuse later.

From Kreshnik's phone, he types a response to Alexa: *Hey. I need to talk to you about Dennis. But not over the phone. Let's meet in person.*

# THIRTY

Alexa juggles three tennis balls in the little front lawn of her townhouse. The neighbors' daughter, an eight-year-old girl, stands beside her, struggling to throw and catch a single ball at a consistent rhythm.

"You're doing great," Alexa says.

The little girl smiles. The ball lands on her shoulder and drops onto the grass.

"Hey Alexa," the girl's father says, wandering out his front door.

"Hey Mister Lewis."

His wife steps outside, walks to Alexa's with her husband. They watch her juggle for a bit. She catches all three balls. They clap.

"How do you like having a little trainee?" the mom asks.

"She's my new bestie."

"You hear that?" the dad says to his daughter. "The cool girl next door thinks you're her bestie."

The child blushes. Alexa gives her a high-five.

"How'd you get into juggling?" the mom asks Alexa.

"My boyfriend took me to one of those Cirque du Soleil shows on the Strip. And this juggler girl was just . . . so good. And I was like, I want to do that. So I bought a pack of tennis balls, watched a couple online tutorials, and started coming out here. Doubt I'll ever get as good as her. But it's fun."

"Well, the fun is unfortunately over for your trainee. She needs to come home for dinner."

"Mom," the little girl says. "A little longer."

"It's okay," Alexa says. "Meet me out here tomorrow."

The little girl collects her tennis ball, waves goodbye, then heads to her house with her parents.

In the grass beside Alexa is her phone. She thinks she heard it ding about a minute ago. Maybe Dennis, who she hasn't heard from in hours, texted her back.

Still so shocking the extent he went to keep her out of prison. Sure, she knew he was okay bending the law. So is she. But kidnapping a federal agent is a butchering of the law.

Her black screen peers up at her. A horror could lurk beneath it, news Dennis did indeed kill that poor FBI agent Jordana.

She takes a deep breath and unlocks her screen.

Yes, she did receive a new text. But not from Dennis. Kreshnik.

He said: *Hey. I need to talk to you about Dennis. But not over the phone. Let's meet in person.*

She puts her palm on her forehead, paces.

She writes back: *Did he go thru w it?*

Him: *Didn't I just tell you not over the phone? Let's discuss in person.*

Her: *Ok fine. Come here.*

Him: *It may not be safe there. Somewhere public nearby. Your pick.*

She sighs.

Her: *Why isn't my place safe?*

Him: *Will explain IN PERSON.*

Her: *Kk. King Lanes bowling alley.*

# THIRTY-ONE

Tommy steps through the glass double-door entrance of King Lanes at the agreed-upon meet time. An Elvis-themed bowling alley off the Strip, the walls covered in murals of the musician in various stage costumes, waitresses zipping by on roller skates, "Hound Dog" on the sound system.

He wears his Lucky Larry's tee shirt, a gash near the bottom from Dennis's knife, still a touch damp. He sits at the bar, orders a club soda.

A pair of spotlight beams oscillates across the twelve lanes. One swings by Tommy, its powerful glare burning his eyes.

He looks away, blinks. The man next to him, alone with a Pabst Blue Ribbon, stares at him.

"Goddamn thing is bright," Tommy says to him.

No reply.

Tommy drinks his club soda for about a minute. The beam passes him again. He kicks his head back, closes his eyes. When he opens them, he notices the bartender peering at him.

"Is the light just part of the deal if you sit on this stool?" Tommy asks.

No reply.

"I can't be the first person to mention this," Tommy says.

The bartender walks away. Tommy moves his stool a foot to the right, reangling himself away from the beam. He gazes at the glass doors. In a bit a blond girl in jean shorts and a tie-dye tee shirt strides through.

Alexa. She folds her arms, clears strands of hair from her eyes. They sweep the room for a man who isn't there.

Tommy pays for his club soda and paces to her. Her gaze swivels to him, apprehension in it.

"Hi Alexa," he says.

Her arms tighten against her chest.

"Kreshnik is dead," he says.

A waitress carrying a tray of burgers and sodas skates around Tommy, blurts, "Keep the server path clear, please."

Tommy moves a couple steps left.

"You're that guy," Alexa says.

"What guy?"

"From the news article. Escaped jail."

"Nice to meet you." A moment. "I'm here because I can help you. And you can help me."

"Where's my brother? What did you force him into? Why—"

"He's okay. He'll be out of the hospital in a couple days. Let's—"

"Hospital?"

156

"Uh . . . he and Kreshnik sort of . . . got into it. But Kurt won. Just a scratch."

She takes a deep breath. "So this was a trick. You're the one who texted me to come here."

"Yes, it was a trick. A well-intentioned one. I'm only here to help—"

"Why do you want to help me? And what makes you think I even need help?"

"Your boyfriend Dennis is a bad guy. I need you to lead me to him."

She laughs. "You getting payback against Dennis for going after your girlfriend might be of interest to you. But not to me."

"The last few days, he put her . . . and me . . . through a lot. So yes, I am out for payback. But this is about you too. You could be in danger."

"You're right, I am in danger. A strange man with a badly sunburnt neck just lured me out of my home."

"I doubt you know what Dennis is capable of."

"I know exactly what he's capable of. Being a loyal boyfriend. I don't know what you're capable of. Which is why I'm leaving." She flashes him a peace sign and meanders through patrons toward the double doors.

He heads after her. His phone vibrates. A new text from Jordan: *We doing dinner or not? Everything ok?*

He veers back into the server path. A waitress stops short on her skates, some beer sloshing out of a pitcher onto his Lucky Larry's shirt.

"Asshole," she says, skating on.

He huffs, puts his phone in his pocket, reminds himself to write Jordana back later. He hustles to Alexa. "I'm just looking to keep you safe. It's what your brother would want."

"A bit presumptuous." She nods at his beer-drenched, sliced shirt. "From what I see, you don't even know how to keep your own clothing safe. What makes you qualified for this? Are you a professional bodyguard?"

"In the spirit of honesty, happy to tell you I'm currently unemployed. My one qualification is I got my girlfriend away from Dennis. When's the last you talked to him?"

"None of your business."

"You know he's been on the run from the feds the last few hours?"

She stops walking. Concern in her expression. "On the run to where?"

"If I knew, I'd be there waiting. Does he love you?"

"That's . . . also none of your business."

"Fine. Tell me anyway. Does he love you?"

"Tell me why you need to know."

"It will determine the rest of your day."

"Ugh. Yes, he loves me. Now what does that determine?"

"Then he's going to come for you. Likely soon. Want you to flee Vegas with him. You agree, you'd be aiding and abetting a high-profile fugitive, expose yourself to a lot more prison time than you already have. You could of course tell him you don't want to go with him. But he seems like the sort of guy who wouldn't take no for an answer. And he's also the sort of guy who hurts women."

Her jaw tightens. "He doesn't hurt women."

"He kidnapped my girlfriend."

"He was just trying to keep me out of prison. He says it's the worst place on earth. Taking your girlfriend was messed up, yes. He just . . . he panicked I guess when he heard I was in trouble."

"He beat her up the night he took her. That was just the beginning. She told me he was planning on cutting her up in his bathtub."

"I don't believe you."

He opens the text conversation on Kreshnik's phone with Dennis, shows the screen to her. "Him and Kreshnik discuss disposal services. AKA, getting rid of a body."

She peeks at the screen, then looks away. "Maybe it means . . . something else, okay? He did legal work too. Maybe they were disposing of . . . legal papers."

"Nothing legal about any of this."

"Well, if Dennis is so bad, I'm sure the FBI will handle him. Don't see why you need me."

"The feds won't protect you. They want you locked up too. But if you stick by me, I'll watch your back. Together we can get to Dennis before them. And I can make sure he's no longer a problem for you."

A moment. "Look . . . I just . . . I don't know about any of this, all right? You showed me a text message that could mean . . . a lot of things. Dennis has been nothing but good to me. Gave me a place to live. Bought me a new phone, new clothes. Took me out to the nicest restaurants on the Strip. Found me a job."

Tommy chuckles. "Blackmailing well-off men at casinos isn't really a job."

She glares at him. "I never force words into their mouths. Don't turn these men into anything they weren't already. All their cheating fantasies come from their own souls. And I never make them true, never hook up with them. Just talk. A lot of them are businessmen in town for conventions. Most brag to me about their work, all their manipulating. How I make my money is a lot purer than how most of them make theirs." A moment. "What are you, like thirty?"

"About. Why?"

"So you got smartphones and social media when

you were already grown up. That stuff was around for people my age since we were babies. We had digital cameras in our faces the moment we were born. We assume everything we do can be recorded. And that's where the world is going whether you like it or not. Way I see it, if some man is worried about a camera out there capturing the real him, instead of fussing about the camera, he should try to fix himself."

Tommy is silent for a bit, the crash of pins around him. "If you want to consider it a job, consider it a job. None of my business. I shouldn't have brought it up. I only care about—"

"It earns me money, so yes, it is a job. But it's more than that. I'm helping these men."

He chuckles. "Just when I was ready to drop this." He runs a hand through his hair. "A guy sending you fifty grand in Bitcoin somehow helps him. I got that right?"

"It's a wake-up call. He pays up, his wife never finds out what he was up to. His marriage stays intact. Hopefully he sees that as an opportunity to appreciate what he has at home, what he almost lost. Or as an opportunity to grow some balls, tell his wife he wants a divorce, and quit sneaking around behind her back."

"An innovative form of marriage counseling. You should tell Doctor Phil. Maybe he—"

"Joke if you want. Won't change the fact I'm right."

"I didn't come here to say if you were right or wrong. I came here to—"

"You're defending these men. By extension, you're telling me I'm wrong."

"I'm not defending them. I'm just . . . I'm—"

"Defending them. The real question is why." She steps closer to him. "Is it because you see a piece of yourself in them?"

He doesn't respond.

She whispers in his ear, "If you were married, on your own in a casino, and I came up to you . . . would you tell me to go away?" She moves her face across his, her lips no more than a half-inch from his, and stares into his eyes waiting for an answer.

He doesn't speak for a few seconds. "What you did at the casinos is in the past. I'm here about your future. To offer you protection."

She smirks. "Thanks for the offer. But I don't need any of your protecting." She walks out the double doors, her blond hair swaying across her tie-dyed back.

# THIRTY-TWO

The dry heat grabs Alexa's face when she exits the bowling alley. She walks to her Chevy Camaro, a twelve-year-old model she purchased a couple weeks ago with her scamming earnings. In middle school, she saw a girl on TV drive a car just like it. And told herself one day she'd have one.

Once she's in the Camaro, out of that Dapino guy's view, no need for her to maintain the guard she had up. She takes a deep breath. A trembling around her ribs.

Dapino's luring her here was of course deceitful, but at least she now knows the truth about Dennis. As she sensed, he lied to her at the townhouse about solving the FBI-agent predicament without violence. Disposal services of course is a euphemism for body dumping.

She collects a half-smoked joint from the glove compartment, sparks it, and takes a long drag. Smoke billows out her lips, a haze overtaking the Camaro. She starts the engine, plays a song from her phone, "Blue Moon Revisited" by Cowboy Junkies.

She pulls out of the lot, the buzz from the weed spreading through her head, which sways to the music. She enters a zone in a corner of her mind that took much practice to create. She started forming this mental place of escape as a kid, when her father would come into her bedroom with the book *Dinosaur Cooking Contest*. He'd slip under the covers to read her the story. But never do much reading.

Her hair dances across her oscillating face. Her eyes close. But she is not scared of a traffic accident. When she is here, she is immune to physical damage. She is all spirit. No body. All spirit. No body.

Her eyes open. She hits the joint again. Thinks about Dennis. When she met him, she was attracted to his fallen-from-grace vibe. A lost-soul former lawyer from the East Coast trying to find his way out in the desert after spending time in prison for a crime he never aimed to commit. It was weird. He was weird. But she's weird too and liked it.

But that must end. She must break up with him. A tear builds in her eye. She dabs it.

After a ten-minute drive, she coasts into Emerald Heights, parks in front of her townhouse. She exits the car, enters the home. Quiet.

After this bizarre day, she craves some comfort food, so walks into the kitchen, opens the pantry, and finds a package of hot chocolate mix in back.

She flips on the stove, the flame providing the only light in the shadowy room, the curtain closed on the window above the sink. She places a pot on the burner, then opens the refrigerator and grabs a carton of milk. Humming, she pours some in the pot. And watches it boil, the marijuana in her making each little bubble interesting.

She grabs a packet of cocoa from the box and starts ripping it open.

In her periphery, she notices someone in the adjoining den.

She gasps, her hands stiffening, brown powder puffing from the packet all over her shirt.

Legs crossed, long hair frazzled, Dennis gazes at her from the couch. "I would like to have a conversation with you."

"Den . . . what . . . uh . . . how did you get in?"

"I own the place, love. I have a key."

An anxious laugh from her. "Right."

"The FBI is after me."

"I know."

"How do you know?"

"I . . . uh . . . I just figured. After what you told me before. About the agent. Only a matter of time, right?"

He rises. And paces to her in the kitchen, his body almost a foot taller than hers. "You are coming with me. Pack a bag. We do not have much time."

She looks down. Notices red splatters on the toes of his boots. "What's that? On your shoes?"

"Ask me anything you want when we are en route." He claps his hands twice. "Grab the essentials. I will buy you new clothing later."

She stares at the shoes. "Can you please explain why you have what appears to be blood on your shoes?"

"Look up at me," he says. She does. "I had to get off the road on my bike. The cops are certainly watching for it. I hid for a while. And needed another vehicle to get to your part of town. I abandoned it about a mile away. The police will not connect us to it. Do not worry."

"So you stole a car? And that's the owner's blood? What did you do to him ... or her?"

He runs his thumb over her chin. "Your beauty is hypnotic. Have I ever told you that?"

She fakes a smile, pretends to check on the heating milk. "I didn't know you were coming. You didn't answer my calls or texts. I would've put on enough for two mugs."

"I had to get rid of that phone. I was fortunately able to acquire a new one when I acquired the car. I spoke to the Albanians. They will help us. We need to go."

"Go where?"

"They agreed to provide me a temporary hideout in town. In exchange for me performing a job for them tonight. Upon its successful completion, they will leverage their network to sneak me out of Nevada, then America. You too."

"This is ... I mean ... it's such short notice. Leave the country?"

He steps closer to her. "We will find a beautiful home in a tropical place. Drinking from coconuts on the beach during the day, dancing in town at night."

She gulps. "Den, I'm ... honored you want to bring me. But we've—"

"Honored? What is this, a Rotary Award acceptance speech?"

"I ... I'm overjoyed. Overjoyed you want to bring me with you. But we've only been dating for what, three months? Running away together is ... it sounds magnificent, don't get me wrong ... but, like also ... you know what I mean?"

"No. Would I ever steer you toward a bad life decision?"

"I know you're always looking out for me. But—"

"You'd still be cleaning up empty beer bottles at Rose Lounge if it weren't for me. You didn't see your potential. You needed me to guide you then. Let me guide you now."

"I like Vegas. Still just settling in. Not ready to move. I—"

"You are still letting that trailer you grew up in weigh you down. When you first got to town, you were elated with your shitty job, your shitty motel room. You needed me to teach you that you deserved better. How good did it feel to punish all those dirty, cheating men and get paid for it?"

She sighs. "How about you give me the night to think about this?"

His long-fingered hand strokes the left side of her body over a tattoo of hers he adores. "Coming here was already a risk. Do not prolong this trip and make me more upset than I already am."

She dips her head, pats his chest. "Okay. Okay. I'll pack a bag."

"Excellent."

She sprints toward the front door.

Three strides. Then she smacks onto the floorboards, his strong grip around her ankle.

"What're you doing?" he screams.

She kicks his head with her free leg. He hunches forward. She reaches for the pot of hot milk on the stove.

Nope. Her arm not long enough.

"Baby," he says.

She kicks him again. Then rips off her tie-dyed tee shirt. And flaps it on the stove flame. The material lights.

"Stop acting crazy," he says, his head lifting.

She whips the fiery shirt at him, torching his hair. He shrieks, letting her go, batting his head with his hands, rolling across the kitchen.

He rushes to the sink, turns on the water. When he leans over to wet his head, the flames meet the curtain over the window.

Alexa dashes into the foyer, snatches her purse from a wall peg, and sprints out the door, nothing on her top half but her lacy black bra and black-stone necklace.

She climbs into her Camaro. Through the front window of the townhouse, the yellows and oranges of a growing blaze.

The car roars onto the road in reverse. A neighbor walking his dog stops and stares. Alexa zooms past him and out of Emerald Heights.

She fumbles for her phone in her purse. And calls Kreshnik's number.

Dapino says on the other line, "What's up?"

"Where are you right now?"

# THIRTY-THREE

Jordana sits in a case room at the FBI's Las Vegas field office, a corkboard on the wall, pinned to it a photo of Dennis Notch surrounded by public record documents of his. Digital-forensics technician Meadows, a chubby Black guy in his thirties with dyed-blond hair, types on a computer beside her.

Waiting for him, she tampers with a paperclip, pulling at the end, twisting the metal into shapes. She used to do this in class at Stanford when she was stressed.

Still no text back from Tommy. Ever since he found her at Dennis's, he's been a bit off. She can't quite pin down why.

Meadows, still typing, says, "Dennis Notch has Visa and AMEX cards in his name." He scrolls down the page on his screen. "The Visa was used last. Today.

Florist on Decatur Boulevard. But that was before he went on the lam."

"With his background as an attorney, he must know what gets fugitives nabbed. I figured he'd be careful."

"Let me see if we've got anything from the airlines. I sent his photo to all that fly out of Vegas and surrounding cities, requesting notification if any of their employees notice a man with his description boarding a plane, regardless of the name on the ticket." He opens a tab on his browser with a table intended to display these notifications.

It's empty.

Jordana sighs. "I need a cup of coffee. You want?"

"I don't drink caffeine. It's bad for you."

"Not in moderation."

"I'm an engineer. I don't do moderation. We're binary. Either all-in on something. Or all-out."

She shrugs, then exits the room toward the kitchen. Blosh, the Vegas Special Agent in Charge, spots her and approaches. "Agent Quick. I was just headed your way."

"What's up?"

"You're going to find this interesting. The accomplice Kurt Thoss killed in the shootout at Dennis Notch's house was named Kreshnik Sulaj. Turns out he had a somewhat noteworthy rap sheet. Last dance was for aggravated assault. While he was working as a bodyguard for Erag Troka."

"Should I know who that is?"

"I suppose they don't have a foothold in San Diego. They've been in LA since the early aughts. Gradually made their way into Vegas. Ramped up quite a bit over the last eighteen months."

"Who?"

"Albanian mafia."

She puts a hand on her hip. "I've read the high-level bureau literature on them. No direct experience."

"The junkyard dogs of the organized crime world. Just as scrappy as they are violent. They have affiliations with the Italians and Russians, often doing the dirty work the big boys don't want to go near."

"And from what I remember, we haven't been able to charge them for much of this dirty work."

"The players are difficult to discern. The Albanians have the hierarchical structure of the Italians, but power isn't aggregated into the hands of a few dons. It's distributed across geographic factions, similar to how the Russians operate. We're pretty confident this fellow Erag Troka heads up an operation in Vegas. But we don't know much about it. Specific streams of revenue, lieutenants, ground presence."

"Also from what I remember, the Albanians are just as bloodline-oriented as the Sicilians. Dennis Notch is a former lawyer from Delaware. He's no gangster. Why is one showing up at his house defending him?"

"You just said it. The lawyer thing, that's my guess. Crime organizations rely on all sorts of paperwork shenanigans to launder money. Gets expensive. Who'd you rather pay for advice, some high-priced guy from one of the corporate firms, or Dennis Notch, who's just as capable but can only charge a fraction without a license?"

"So we've got a squeaky clean Ivy League kid from a well-off suburb. Goes to prison. And comes out a mob lawyer, scam artist, kidnapper, and potential murderer."

"He played by the rules his whole life and that landed him in a concrete box. When he got out, he probably decided the rules weren't for him anymore."

"The Albanians could be hiding him. Send me everything we have on their Vegas operation, regardless of how limited."

Meadows walks over. "Agent Quick?"

Jordana and Blosh turn to him. "Change your mind about the coffee?" she asks.

"No. I just got a call from Metro PD. The fire department is putting out a pretty bad one at the Emerald Heights development. A witness walking his dog saw two people run out of the townhouse, one after the other. No more than twenty minutes ago. A petite blonde in her twenties. And a tall man with dark hair in his thirties."

"Alexa and Dennis," Blosh says.

Jordana jogs toward Meadows. "Take me to Emerald Heights."

# THIRTY-FOUR

Tommy paces his Bonanza Inn room anticipating Alexa's arrival. Memories of her at the bowling alley flicker in his mind. Her legs in those jean shorts. Her blue eyes. Her pouty lips.

Yes, he loves Jordana. And yes, he finds Alexa attractive. In a perfect world, both couldn't be true at the same time. But as Tommy knows, this is not a perfect world.

His gaze jumps to a row of mini booze bottles on the dresser beside a spread of local magazines, on the top one's cover a theater performer swallowing a sword. He unscrews a Jack Daniel's bottle and gulps.

After a couple more swigs, the little bottle is empty. He tosses it in the trash, goes to unscrew a Jim Beam one. But no. He can't cloud his mind with too much alcohol on his hunt for Dennis. He chucks the

Jim Beam in the corner, out of his reach. Hands on his hips, he stares at the rug.

A light knock from the hallway. He opens the door. Alexa stands before him, still in her jean shorts, her skin wicked in a light sweat. Her shirt is gone, nothing on her top half but a bra and necklace, a tattoo running from her left hip up her side that says in script *Edge of Chaos*.

"They let you in wearing that?" he asks.

"It's a cheap motel in Vegas. I used to live in one. They've seen a lot less." She brushes past him and sits on the bed.

"Let me, uh, let me get you something." He closes the door, steps into the bathroom, and returns with a towel. He drapes it over her shoulders, covering her cleavage.

"Thanks."

"Yeah. Look, here's what I'm thinking . . . call Dennis, tell him you forgive him for the fight at your place, that you want to make up. Pick a place to meet. I'll be there waiting."

"He didn't give me a new number. And his old one—"

"Yeah, I know about his old one." An audible exhale from Tommy.

"I can try emailing him."

"Can't hurt. But after all he's done, the feds may have authorization to monitor his personal account. He probably knows that and would avoid logging in. Same with social media. Did he ever mention any sort of a meetup hideout for you two, like out in the desert, in case of an emergency?"

"No, never. You sure they didn't already catch him after the fire? Police must've shown up. Whatever car he had was apparently a mile away. They could've seen him when he was on foot."

"Nah, my girlfriend would've told me the news. Speaking of which, I've got to text her back." He steps toward his phone on the night table.

"Well, then he's gotta be with the Albanians."

He stops before grabbing his phone. "What Albanians?"

"Kreshnik's . . . people."

"Kreshnik had family in town?"

"No, not family in the traditional way."

Tommy flashes her a confused squint.

"Oh come on," she says. "You're from New York. You must be familiar with this type of thing."

"What?"

"Who did you think Kreshnik was?"

"Some 'roided-up friend Dennis called over for muscle."

"Yeah, fine. But that's not all. And the thing I do at the casinos with Dennis isn't the only way he makes money. Like I mentioned, he does lawyer paperwork. For Kreshnik's . . . people." She adjusts the towel over her shoulders. "Albanian mafia."

Tommy leans against the wall. He's of course familiar with the Italian and Russian mob. And yes, he's heard of an Albanian version, but knows almost nothing about them. He's silent for a bit.

"What?" she asks.

"The mob . . . the mob makes this a whole different beast." He rubs his temples. "Tell me about these guys."

"I can't. Never met them, just Kreshnik. He and Dennis were more than business acquaintances. Actual friends. We got drinks with him and his girlfriend a couple times. She was nice. So was he. I can't believe Kurt . . . killed him. Kurt. Damn."

"If you don't know these other men, why're you so

confident Dennis is with them now?"

"Before. He mentioned a thing he's doing with them. Tonight."

"What thing?"

"Just . . . a job, he said."

Tommy scratches his chin.

"Are you disappointed I don't have more for you?" she asks.

"No. You're fine." A moment. "It's just . . . Vegas is a big town. Must be a million shadowy crevices he could be holed up. Especially if they're helping hide him."

She nudges back on the bed cross-legged. "Well, maybe that's good. If he stays in some crevice, he'll be away from me."

"Not necessarily true. If he's in with the mob, he has access to their resources. He could send someone to . . . bring you to him."

Her face loses some color. "Really?"

"Why not?"

"But he has no idea where I am."

Tommy moves the curtain to the side, scans the parking lot for anyone suspicious, a couple fast food joints in the background. "That can always change." He closes the curtain.

"Ugh." She drops her back onto the bed. Her eyes settle on the Jim Beam bottle in the corner. "I can use a fucking drink."

He picks it up, hands it to her.

"What was it doing on the floor?" she asks, unscrewing the cap.

"Maybe the maid . . . knocked it over. You want anything to eat? I'm starving."

"I'm okay. Just . . . do me a favor. Don't pick up from one of those fast food restaurants across the street. I don't like being around that stuff when people eat it."

"What's your beef with fast food places?"

She rolls her eyes. "Was that supposed to be a . . . what do you call it? A pun?"

"Good one, right?"

"I saw this documentary once about what goes on with all the animals that those places use to make food. The cows and chickens. It was really disturbing. They're bred for certain characteristics, bigger parts of the body where they get the meat from. And once they're born, their whole life is mapped out for them. They're on this inevitable path, being sorted, bulked up, then slaughtered. And you see them in the movie . . . you know . . . like eating their grass or seeds or whatever and they don't even know. Don't even know what they were born into."

"Pizza it is." He does a Google search on his phone for local pizzerias. She turns on the TV, flips through the channels while he orders.

When done, he drifts toward her, stands by the bed watching an episode of *Frasier* she put on.

"I love this show," she says. "Ever watch it?"

"Not really."

"The brother, the brother's my favorite."

A joke is delivered, laughter from the studio audience. Tommy, who missed the setup, doesn't get it, but Alexa does, giggling. A little clap of her hands under the towel.

Just a couple minutes ago she had a fearing-for-her-life demeanor. Now a big grin, engrossed in a show. He's never met another person with the ability to move from one extreme to another in such an effortless manner. He isn't sure if it's a good trait or bad.

They watch TV for about a half hour. The pizza shows up. Tommy sets it beside her on the bed, bites into a slice. It does not taste like New York pizza. Not even as good as the stuff he gets in San Diego. But he's so hungry the slice goes down in about five seconds.

A knock at the door.

Alexa must read surprise in his expression because a look of caution overtakes hers. He paces to the door. And peers through the peephole.

A feeling of dread hits him.

# THIRTY-FIVE

Tommy can avoid this. Another knock on the door. He remains silent, trying to give the impression nobody is in here. Another knock.

"Babe?" Jordana says from the hallway. "I've been texting you."

"What's wrong?" Alexa asks.

Shit. He presses his finger to his lips, signaling for her to be quiet.

"Hello?" Jordana says. "I heard someone. Who's in there?"

Now he can't avoid this. He takes a deep breath, glimpses Alexa on the bed. Not a good picture. But he did nothing wrong. Not a thing. He can explain himself.

He opens the door with a smile. "Hey sweetie."

Jordana maneuvers past him as if determined to

see the owner of the feminine voice.

Her feet freeze. Her eyes bulge taking in Alexa.

Neither girl speaks for a few seconds. Jordana lets out a laugh. Contempt in it. "Oh," she says. "Oh, wow. This . . . I've seen a lot as an FBI agent, but I didn't expect this."

"It isn't what it looks like," Tommy says.

"It looks like a half-naked girl is on your bed. Not just any half-naked girl, but a professional slut."

"Come on."

"That's how she makes her money. Where did you meet her? How?"

"She doesn't . . . she didn't sleep with the guys at the casinos."

"What're you now, Tommy, her fucking attorney? She has you on retainer with her dirty money? What is going on?"

"She didn't . . . hire me for anything. How about—"

"So if she isn't here for business, what then . . . pleasure?"

"Jordana, please."

"You, please. Where's her shirt?"

"She lost it getting away from Dennis."

Jordana steps closer to him, glaring. "Even if that's true, which I doubt, why would she leave Dennis and end up in a motel room with you?"

"So I could keep her safe from him. A promise to her brother."

"You knew I've been looking for her. You didn't care to tell me you found her?"

"I didn't . . . I didn't think you guys would treat her nicely."

"No kidding. She's wanted for federal blackmail."

"Exactly."

"Oh, no, no, no. Don't exactly me."

"I'm not trying to start a fight here."

"Then you probably should've reconsidered the half-naked whore on the bed."

He rubs his shoulder. "I . . . I'm also doing this for you. I hope you realize that."

She thumps her foot. "This whole thing I walked in on, this was set up for my benefit?"

"Yes."

"So you ignore my texts because you're in bed with her, but I—"

"I wasn't in bed with her," he yells, banging his fist against the wall.

Silence for a second.

"Dennis Notch attacked you," he says. "Chained you. And threatened to cut you up. You know me enough to know I want to get my hands on him for that. Don't you?"

She looks away.

"I wanted to find Dennis Notch on my own," he says, "not drag you into it, not get you in trouble at work. That's why I've been avoiding your texts. Sorry. Alexa is my source of info. That's all that's going on here."

Jordana's eyes flick to Alexa, then back to him. "I don't buy it."

A hollow laugh from him. "Well, guess I can't do anything about that."

"No. Guess you can't."

"I saved your life today. And this is the thanks I get? Why'd you even come here? Because I didn't reply to your texts right away? A little extreme?"

"No, you dick. I came here because I know Blosh won't let me discuss the case with you at the office. But I respect your opinion. And wanted it regardless. I have a new strategy. Stopped by to show some supporting details to you, see what you thought. The front desk gave me your room number when I flashed my badge."

He feels the red of embarrassment on his cheeks. "Oh. All right, then. I'd love to hear your strategy." He pulls over a chair for her. "We were just discussing angles for finding Dennis too. What do—"

Jordana laughs. "I respected your opinion before, not anymore. Not after this vomit of lies."

"I'm not lying."

"Did you hook up with her?"

"No."

She studies his eyes. "I still don't believe you."

"We didn't," Alexa says.

Jordana scowls at her. "Nobody asked you anything. Shut your whore mouth."

"Please don't call me a whore."

"I can call you whatever I want. Do you know who I am?"

"Yeah. And I know you had a hard day. I'm sorry for what Dennis did to you. I was not in on it. But don't take that out on Tommy. He's been nothing but a gentleman."

Jordana steps to the bed, leans over inches from Alexa. "Let me tell you a little secret, Alexa. In America, we like saying how everyone is created equal. But that's a bunch of horseshit. The better people succeed. And they create kids better than the others. And the cycle continues. I come from the good kind of people. But you? I've been to your family's trailer. Seen what you're from. Know the loser gene pool that spat you out. You may have gotten out of Willince, but you'll always be trash."

A silence hangs in the room for a few seconds.

"Give me all the shit you want," Tommy says in a

low voice. "Leave her out of this. Please."

Jordana turns to him. "No, you're the one who'll leave her out of this. Pick. Right now."

"Pick what?"

"Tell her to leave the motel. And I'll . . . take that as proof this wasn't anything romantic. And we'll get past it. Or don't. And I'm the one who'll be leaving. And I promise you I won't be looking back on this relationship."

"Whoa. Let's just—"

"Her or me, Tommy?"

He takes a deep breath. His gaze moves from one girl to the other, passing over the painting of the gas station in the desert dusk.

"How am I supposed to live with myself if I let her go and Dennis hurts her?" Tommy asks.

Jordana nods. "Okay. I have your decision. Her." She marches out of the room. The door slams on Tommy and Alexa.

# THIRTY-SIX

Dennis sits in the backseat of a Mercedes G-Wagon idling in the corner of a convenience store's parking lot, the side windows tinted, his face obscured from view.

Lingering around him is the scent of his own burnt hair. A clump of it seared off the left side of his head, a patch of reddish scalp showing, burns streaking that side of his face, the eye oozing puss.

An Albanian gangster, a mid-thirties pretty boy who only goes by the nickname Cameroon Joe, sits in the driver's seat. Feathered hair, tucked-in silk button-down, dark sunglasses. He drove Dennis here after the fire at Alexa's, scooped him up from his hiding spot, a Porta-Potty on a nearby construction site.

A white Bentley pulls next to them. A pudgy, five-foot-two man steps out and climbs into the passenger seat of the Mercedes. Erag Troka, early fifties, the head of the Albanian mafia's Vegas faction.

Troka gazes at Dennis, cringes at his charred face. Cameroon Joe chuckles, says, "Looks like he was rim jobbing a blowtorch, huh boss?"

"That's not funny," Troka says, his voice deeper than his height suggests. He sets his palm on Dennis's knee. "Are you in pain, son?"

"Yes. But I have more important things to worry about than physical pain."

"Want something to put on your fried face? Like an ointment." Troka turns to Cameroon Joe. "Do you carry ointment?"

"What makes you assume that?"

"You're one of those guys into taking care of himself."

"My appearance. Ointment's not for your appearance."

"Hmm. Moisturizer, then. That is. This guy's face can use some moisture."

"Sorry boss. I keep mine in my bathroom. Carrying it around would be weird."

A pause. "You know who's weird? Jetmir."

"I know. I saw him once eat Doritos with a fork. Not a plastic one. Metal."

"You think a metal fork makes it weirder than plastic?"

"Yeah. More ... formal."

"Mmm." Troka turns to Dennis. "Ointment is out."

"I will be fine."

Troka purses his lips. "You don't look fine. You sure you're all right to do a job for me?"

"My spirits may be subpar right now, but I assure you, sir, my mind is sound. What is this job?"

"Something I've been planning for a while. It

involves negotiation. I was going to do that part myself. But then remembered I have a Georgetown lawyer on my payroll. This will be a perfect last task before we get you off the grid."

"Negotiating is my specialty. But there is one more thing. My girlfriend."

"What about her?"

"I cannot leave the country without her."

"The one who lit you on fire?"

Cameroon Joe snickers.

"I . . . yes . . . I know she lit me on fire," Dennis says. "She is just confused. Young. Often does not understand what is best for her. Being with me is best for her. She will eventually see that."

Troka sighs. "You've had your fun with this broad. Leave her behind. Find a new one when you're settled in your new city. Find ten new ones."

"With all due respect, sir, you do not understand. She is not just some floozy I had fun with. I love her."

Dennis thinks back to his first date with Alexa. They met for pizza. Talked about their favorite documentaries. He asked her if she'd like to go for a drink. Then took her to the nicest bar at The Venetian. They split a bottle of champagne at two thirty in the afternoon. Then another. Soon they were back at his place.

Tipsy, she said he made her comfortable and opened up about her overbearing mother. He had more to drink, told her she made him comfortable too, and admitted to his stint in prison. Mentioned it was hard on him. Without him realizing, a tear came from his eye. He tried to hide it, but she saw. He waited for her to make an excuse and leave in pity. Instead she kissed him.

"Every cop and fed in Nevada is after you," Troka says. "Bringing this girl into our mix creates an extra variable nobody needs."

Dennis is quiet for a while. "When I was in prison I punched a guard. And did thirty days in solitary. Toward the end, I grew tired of eating. Drinking water too. I slipped into a different mental state. Maybe I was hallucinating, but I felt extreme harmony. Like I was speaking to God. And he told me I was to be sent this perfect girlfriend after I got out. And she would make up for all the bad that has happened to me. She would make everything all right."

Cameroon Joe chuckles. "It definitely sounds like God gave you a relationship with plenty of heat."

"Enough," Troka says. He looks at Dennis. "What do you want from me here?"

"After my little misunderstanding with Alexa, she would run if I approached her. Plus, coming out of hiding would be risky. I need you to bring her to me. Without hurting her."

A loud exhale from Troka's nose. "This job I have for you will demand your full attention. I arranged a safe location where you can operate. One of our businesses you did the paperwork for. When the job is done, we can discuss reuniting you with your little valentine."

Dennis smiles.

# THIRTY-SEVEN

Alexa, her top half still in just a bra and necklace, waits in the driver's seat of her Camaro, parked in an illegal zone, while Tommy steps out and enters a touristy apparel shop across from the Mirage, dozens of electric billboards shining in a foggy sky on the edge of day and night.

In a few minutes he walks back to the car, sticks a plastic bag through the window. She pulls out a white tee shirt with an image of dice, *Viva Las Vegas* underneath.

"Styling," she says.

He says nothing back. Leans against the side of the car, gazes at the mishmash of passersby, a mime among them street performing. While Alexa puts on the shirt, Tommy opens Jordana's Facebook page on his phone, navigates to a photo of her and her family in matching fleeces with their wine company's name, *Velatti*, stitched on their chests, their vineyard behind them. Every Christmas the extended Velatti family poses for the same picture, one of their many traditions.

He could've been in these photos going forward, Jordana's husband. Soon, their kids would've appeared. Those lush green hills behind them, a backdrop quite different than the neighborhood in Queens where he grew up.

In her *Viva Las Vegas* shirt, Alexa steps around the front of the car. Tommy closes Facebook.

"If you just want to go home after everything that happened at the motel," she says, "I'd understand. Don't force yourself to stay here because of me."

"What happened at the motel was ultimately your boyfriend's fault. None of—"

"Ex-boyfriend."

"Anyway, none of us would be in this mess if it weren't for him. I'm not going back to San Diego. I have an ex too because of him. I want to bury him now even more than before." He removes Kreshnik's phone from his pocket. "Speaking of which, I have a plan."

"You came up with that pretty fast. Kinda impressed."

"Only be impressed if it works." He taps a few buttons on the phone. "Now that I know Kreshnik was in the mob, and they're likely guarding Dennis, figured his phone could imply a hideout." He shows her the screen. An online listing for a business called E-Z Ship. "Kreshnik ever mention this place?"

"Shipping store, North Vegas? No."

"Well, according to the Waze app on his phone, he went here pretty often."

"Maybe he sold stuff on eBay for extra money.

Why would Dennis be there?"

Tommy expands a street-view photo of E-Z Ship. "Look at this joint. In a dingy strip mall. Sign barely noticeable. This isn't a store aimed at real customers."

"So, it goes after fake ones?"

"It's a front."

Her expression indicates she doesn't know what that is.

"They're a common tactic in organized crime," he says. "Companies that exist just for washing money."

Her expression still confused.

"It's a way to make illegal income look legit," he says.

"Ah, like my townhouse. Former townhouse. Dennis mentioned something like that about it. Was sort of boring, so I stopped listening after he told me I didn't need to pay rent."

"Wouldn't surprise me if Dennis was using that asset to wash money. The Albanians are likely doing the same with this shipping store. Meaning they control it. Meaning Dennis might be hiding there. Ideal place. Outskirts of town. Inconspicuous. Not a lot of visitors. I want to go check."

A moment. "By now, these mafia guys probably know you had something to do with Kreshnik's death. If you show up to one of their . . . front businesses . . . looking around, asking questions, they're going to get suspicious. And you're probably going to get hurt."

"That's where you come in."

"Me?"

"I can't do this alone."

She taps the side of her face with her index finger a couple times. "What're you suggesting?"

"If he's there, he'll be hiding in a private section. You distract whoever's upfront while I sneak into the back."

"Distract how?"

"You're a professional con artist. I'm sure you can think of something."

She takes a deep breath. Then nods and gets back into the Camaro. He sits in the passenger seat. She drives toward the shipping store, maneuvering through the heavy traffic. He gazes at the Strip lights piercing the fog.

"The Facebook photo you picked was interesting," she says.

He clicks on his seatbelt. "You spying on me?"

"Wasn't trying to be nosey or anything. You had it open when I walked over."

"Well, it's not open anymore."

"In the news article I read about her disappearing, they had a paragraph on her family. Her real last name. Velatti. I've heard of it. The wine. She must be loaded."

"They're not poor."

"I don't think you were dating her for money though."

"I wasn't. Some people have a hard time believing that."

"If you were after her dough, you'd want to have the prenup conversation as soon as possible to see if you were wasting your time. You haven't had the conversation yet."

"How'd you know that?"

"If you had it, one of two things would've happened immediately after. If you were happy with the conversation, you would've proposed. And she would've had a ring on her finger. Which I did not notice. If you were not happy with the conversation, you would've broken up with her. Which of course never happened. As I witnessed, she was the one who broke up with you."

"Huh. Not bad."

"Bringing me back to the Facebook photo. It's not her family money you feel you're missing out on. But her family itself. Am I right?"

"I . . . can we not talk about this?"

Silence for a few seconds.

"My mom used to be a pretty normal, nice person," she says. "After my dad . . . left, she stopped caring about certain things. Like family events. Birthdays included. My best friend at the time, Daisy, she had a big family. Both parents home, two brothers, two sisters. They didn't live in a trailer. They lived in a house. Wasn't fancy or anything. But it was a real house. With nice, fresh towels in the bathroom. And a new TV. And like those little canvas signs with cute quotes on them."

"Why're we talking about this again?"

"Hear me out. On my birthday, sometimes my mom would give me a dinky gift, like a pack of candy, other years nothing. At night though, I would go to Daisy's. And her family, all through middle school, they'd make me a big cake. And get me two presents. Real presents, not candy. One would be from Daisy, the other from the rest of them. And after we had cake, we'd all go into the den and play boardgames till late, like eleven."

"Daisy's family sounds cool."

"They were. Until birthdays there stopped."

"What happened? They moved or something?"

"My mom is what happened." A moment. "When I was a freshman in high school, a couple days before my birthday, she tells me she didn't want me going over to Daisy's anymore. Said she heard Daisy's dad,

Mister Belle, was having an affair with some hooker."

"How did she stumble on that tidbit?"

"She didn't. Mister Belle couldn't have had a better relationship with Mrs. Belle. My mom definitely made it up. Soon the rumor spread all over town."

"Why the hell would she do that?"

"She couldn't stand what him and his wife had. And that I liked being with them more than her. It was her attempt at making the Belles and me just as miserable as she was. They got through it. But I of course didn't. No more invitations to the house on birthdays. Or ever."

"I'm, uh, that sucks, Alexa."

"So . . . my point is, I get it. Jordana. Her family. Maybe they were your Belles. If so, it hurts when that gets ripped away from you."

He glimpses the profile of her youthful face, then gazes back out at the fog. He tries not to think of everything he lost when Jordana walked out the motel room door. He must focus on the plan against the Albanians. If he doesn't, he is sure to lose something else. His life.

# THIRTY-EIGHT

Dennis, head in his hands, sits in front of a desk in the office of one of the money laundering businesses the Albanian mob runs in Vegas, the boss, Troka, across from him munching on a bag of Skittles. On the wall behind him is a motivational poster of racecar driver Jeff Gordon.

"I am not comfortable doing this," Dennis says.

"We had a deal. I shelter you, get you out of the States, in exchange for you helping me on a job."

"Before we made the deal, you did not tell me what the job entailed."

"It entails negotiation. Your self-proclaimed specialty."

"It also entails mass death."

"Only if the hotel doesn't comply. You did time for manslaughter. I didn't think you were so sensitive."

"I was walking to my car at night and two Black men started following me. They were toying with me, telling me how nice my watch looked, telling me they couldn't wait to see what car I stopped at. I told them to let me be. When they refused, I threw a punch. Knocked the bigger one in the jaw. He slipped on ice, fell, broke his neck. A traffic camera recorded it. Prosecutor made it look like a hate crime. Which it wasn't. I'm no killer. I was just unfortunate."

"Weren't you and Kreshnik about to chop up an FBI agent today?"

"I . . . well . . . that was more misfortune. See, I didn't want to kill her. But that was the only way. I had no choice."

"You have no choice now either."

"There must be some other job you could use me on."

Troka tosses a big handful of Skittles in his mouth. Chewing, he says, "If I turned you in to the FBI, I'd probably gain a big bargaining chip. Which I could cash in if I ever got into a pickle." He swallows. "Maybe I'm looking at this dynamic between me and you from the wrong angle."

Dennis runs his tongue over his teeth a few times. "Fine. Fuck it. Fine."

"Skittle?"

"No thank you."

Troka sends a text message. In about a half hour, he receives one, then motions Dennis to sit next to him behind the desk. Dennis drags his chair over and, with his non-burnt eye, gazes at a laptop screen. On it two live video feeds, one from a small camera clipped to Cameroon Joe's shirt, the second a similar camera on a late-twenties woman named Drita, Troka's niece.

Cameroon Joe enters the lobby of the Hyacinth

Hotel, Vegas's newest luxury resort. A blown glass sculpture on the ceiling, elaborate floral arrangements the floor. Like all modern Vegas destinations, it is wired with a cutting-edge security system. And, according to Troka, Cameroon Joe is carrying in an illicit item.

If it were already put together, Troka informed, an X-ray scanner would notice it. So Cameroon Joe takes it in disassembled, the parts distributed in two leather bags, one in each hand.

He strides through the casino past a cluster of roulette tables and slips into a bathroom, one of the few places where surveillance cameras are prohibited. He steps inside an unoccupied stall, sets the two overnight bags atop the toilet, and flashes a thumbs-up at his body camera.

Troka calls Drita. She picks up. He says, "Third stall from the entrance," and hangs up. Dennis's functioning eye goes to her video feed. According to Troka, she is dressed in a Hyacinth maid outfit, with a prosthetic nose, red wig, and blue contacts. She pushes a cleaning cart through a hallway.

She passes through double doors onto the casino floor and moves toward the men's room adjacent to the roulette tables. Once there, she situates a yellow A-frame sign in front of the entrance labeled *Closed for Cleaning.*

She goes in, tells the half-dozen men to please leave. Then steps into the third stall, grabs Cameroon Joe's pieces of luggage, and conceals both in the trash bag of her maid cart.

"She's a good kid, isn't she?" Troka asks.

Dennis grins, his charred skin hurting from the facial movement.

Drita pretends to clean the bathroom for a couple minutes, then slips the A-frame onto her cart and approaches the elevators to the guestrooms.

She boards one and holds up to a sensor a maid's universal keycard, supplied by a real hotel maid along with the uniform, both yielded from a healthy bribe from Troka.

Drita rises to the twentieth story. Pushing the cart, she advances through a corridor with abstract art canvases lining the wall.

"That one's nice," Troka says as she passes a painting of gray splotches over yellow circles. "It reminds me of my grandmother's smile." He pops a couple Skittles in his mouth.

Drita moseys by a couple doors with *Do Not Disturb* signs on the handles. She stops at another without one. Knocks. The door doesn't open. She slips the universal keycard in a slot, gains access.

A sweeping view of the Strip outside floor-to-ceiling windows. Scattered clothing on a couch, bedsheets ruffled.

She flips on the lights, removes Cameroon Joe's bags from the cart, and empties the contents. A box of nails, a box of ball bearings, an electric switch, a pressure cooker, among other material for assembling an IED, AKA an improvised explosive device.

Or the more common term, a bomb.

With careful hands, she pieces together the components. Like bathrooms, guestrooms lack surveillance, no cameras or X-rays in here, Dennis and Troka the only people watching her commit the deed.

Once she's done, she activates the bomb, a timer on it counting down to midnight. She tucks it in the back of the closet and snaps a photo. Then stashes the empty luggage on the cart and leaves.

"That's my girl," Troka says. He turns to Dennis,

hands him a cellphone. "As the Americans say, you're up to bat."

# THIRTY-NINE

Alexa opens the door of North Vegas's E-Z Ship store, two tiny bells attached to it jingling. The place looks like a small, dated version of a FedEx Office. It's empty other than a late-thirties man behind the counter, comb-over on a balding head, the arc of a beer gut underneath an Adidas tee shirt.

His eyes take in Alexa. "Yo," he says in an accent that sounds like Kreshnik's.

She smiles. "Yo."

"Can I help you?"

She walks past two printers, a shelf of cardboard boxes, reams of paper, and packaging tape. "I'm not here to buy anything."

"Then what's a girl like you doing in a part of town like this?"

"So sorry for just like barging in here."

"No problem."

"My car. I can't get it to start. I know nothing about engines or stuff like that. And I used to have Triple A. Then canceled for some reason. And I'm just ... ugh. You know?"

"Totally."

"I noticed you through the window. You looked like the type of guy who's good with cars."

"I know my way around a transmission or two."

She curls a strand of hair around her finger. "You don't seem busy. Mind having a quick look under my hood?"

He taps the glass counter, rattling the pens and pair of scissors in a pencil cup. "Where's your car?"

"In the lot, literally right outside your door. If I see a customer come through it while you're looking at my engine, I'll tell you." She points at the Camaro on the other side of the window.

"Why not?" He steps around from behind the counter.

"Oh my God. You're my hero. Like ... wow."

They walk outside into the lot. He asks her to pop her hood. While he examines the engine, she notices Tommy skulk around the corner of the strip mall and slip through the front door of the shop.

"Is it making a noise or anything when you try to start it?" the attendant asks.

"Yeah. It almost sounds like a bird."

"Like a squawk?"

"Sorta."

"Huh. That is odd. But I think I know what it could be." He plays around with the intricate metal machinery for a while. "How about you get behind the wheel and give it a shot? Let me hear."

"Sure." She climbs in the driver's seat. Starts the

engine. It sounds fine. "How do you like that?" she says out the open door with a smile.

"Something must've been lodged in there. Looks like I knocked it out of place. Told you I knew what it was."

"Like I said. My hero."

Her phone, on the seat beside her, vibrates. A text from Tommy: *Bring him back inside.*

"My pleasure," the shop attendant says.

"Now that I'm here, I actually could use some boxes. Have to ship some internet returns."

"Yeah. I got all kinds of boxes."

She kills the engine, climbs out of the car, and saunters toward the store, the man at her side.

"So what does a girl like you do for fun?" he asks.

"I'm a homebody. Don't go out a lot."

He opens the shop door. "That's a shame." They enter.

Tommy bursts out from behind a printer. His arm wraps the attendant's neck. The guy flails.

"What the hell are you doing?" Alexa asks Tommy.

"Finding Dennis here was plan A. I looked. He's not here. This is plan B."

"Who the fuck are you?" the guy asks.

With a swift motion of his leg, Tommy kicks his feet out, then leads him to the floor and pins his knee into the center of his back.

"You don't know who you're screwing with," the guy says, struggling to break free.

"Albanian mob. I don't have a problem with you or your crew. I'm looking for your lawyer. Dennis Notch."

The guy stares up at Tommy. "You motherfucker. I saw your picture online. You killed Kreshnik."

"Not technically. And besides, Kreshnik tried to kill me first. None of that matters now." Tommy digs his knee harder into his back. "From what I heard, the Albanians play nice with the Italians and Russians. But not the Mexicans. On the way over here I saw a few Latinos with gang ink hanging out on a sidewalk." He points at a roll of packaging tape. "Maybe I tape you up, tell them you're in here. And you can see how fast all your shit gets robbed."

"What do you want from me?"

"Where's Dennis?"

"I'm on counter duty, man. Do I seem like the sort of dude who talks to the lawyers? I have no idea."

"Maybe your boss does. Hit him up and ask. Or else this place gets cleaned out and you look like a jackass who can't watch his post."

"My boss is going to want to know why I'm interested in Dennis's location."

Tommy thinks for a moment. "Tell him Dennis's girlfriend came in looking for him. Needs his address. Which is actually true."

"This chick is really Dennis's girlfriend?"

"Ex. If you don't believe me, take a photo of her. Send it to your boss. Have him pass it to Dennis to confirm. Dennis will happily give up his address for her. And you can play dumb about the rest. Do that and I let you go."

The guy huffs. "Fine asshole. Give me my phone. Back pocket."

Tommy fishes it out of his jeans, hands it to him. Scowling, the attendant snaps a picture of Alexa, then sends it and a message to the contact *Jetmir*.

# FORTY

"Hyacinth Resort and Casino, this is Katie, how may I assist you?" the twenty-three-year-old female concierge says into a phone in her Minnesota accent.

Sitting between two others at a long marble desk just off a group of slots, she wears a pencil skirt and blouse with a *Katie* nametag. When she started the job, it said *Katelyn*, but she suggested the casual version would make her more approachable to guests. Her boss not only agreed, but recommended the casual policy throughout the service division.

The guest on the phone asks Katie for a good steakhouse recommendation. She gives him one right here on the property, makes him a nine PM reservation.

"Anything else I can help you with, Mister Ligurst?" she asks. He says no. "All right. And remember, they're known for the tomahawk for two. But only if you and your wife have the appetite. Hope you skipped lunch." A half-chuckle from her. "So long, sir."

She hangs up. Gazes out at the TV-show-themed slot machines, waiting for her next call. Within seconds, it comes.

She picks up. "Hyacinth Resort and Casino, this is Katie, how may I assist you?"

"There is a bomb in the hotel," a male voice says. "And it will go off at midnight unless I am sent ten million dollars in Bitcoin."

She says nothing. The two other concierges at her sides, both on calls, sound ten times farther from her than they did seconds ago. Katie closes her eyes. An image flashes among the blackness. That man in the gray suit who spoke to her class of new hires during employee orientation three weeks ago.

This was part of the training. A bomb scare. A process is in place. If she just follows the process, everything will be okay.

"I understand, sir," she says, her voice quaky but coherent. "I'm going to put you on hold for just a second, then come back on and listen to everything you have to say."

She presses a mute button on the console.

"What's going on?" the girl to her left asks.

Katie, her head dizzy, ignores her. She springs up from her seat and yanks open a drawer. The man in the gray suit mentioned what she needs would be in here. She searches, can't find it. Maybe it was the other drawer.

"You all right, Katie?" her colleague asks.

No reply. She scans the labels on the manila folders in the second drawer. And spots *DHS*, the acronym for Department of Homeland Security.

She rummages through the files until locating one titled *Bomb Threat Checklist* and sits back in her chair.

She unmutes the phone, says into it, "Okay sir . . . what else would you like me to know?"

"Nothing," the caller says, his voice now with a Scottish accent, maybe due to some sound-masking software. "When can I expect the money?"

She reads the first question on the checklist, asks it to him, "Where is the bomb located?"

"That is of no concern to you," the caller says, his pace slowing, his pronunciation elongating into a Southern drawl.

"Okay. Well, when will the bomb go off?"

"That is also of no concern to you."

"What . . . uh . . . what does it look like?"

"I shall save you the time. I know all the questions on the DHS checklist. And I know I will not be answering any."

"Oh."

"Would you like to call the police, dear?"

"Should I call the police?" A moment. "No. Why would you want me to call the police? Is that a trick question?" She feels her eyes watering.

"You can call the police if you choose. But if I sense you did, I will set the explosive off. And you will be forever burdened with the maimings and murders that result. You have a young voice. Many years to live. Many decades for the names of the dead and disfigured to haunt you. Why would you want that, Katie?"

"No." She clears her throat. "I don't want that."

"Though I am sure the concierge can arrange for me fantastic seats at a show tonight," he says, now in a female voice, "I have no expectations you can arrange my ten million dollars. Am I correct, darling?"

"Yeah . . . yes. That's correct."

"I will call back in exactly sixty minutes. Within that time, speak to your boss, then your boss's boss, and however many bosses you need to until reaching someone who can authorize my payment. I expect to converse with this person then. Bye Katie."

He ends the call.

# FORTY-ONE

Tommy still has his knee on the back of the attendant at E-Z Ship. Alexa sealed the shop's blinds, spun the *Open* sign to *Closed*, and locked the door to deter a customer from stumbling in.

A metallic clank by the entrance, someone trying to open the door. Another clank. A male voice outside says, "Guzim?"

The attendant looks toward it.

"Guzim?" the man says outside, his fist banging the door. "You there?"

The attendant's phone, on the rug beside his face, vibrates. On the screen, a new text message from the contact *Jetmir: I was in the area. Stopped by to discuss in person. Here now. Where the fuck did you go?*

The boss.

If they don't open the door, his suspicion will only

escalate. No way he'll text Dennis's address. They need to confront this problem head on.

Tommy waves Alexa to him, whispers in her ear, "Let him in. Try to get Dennis's location off him." Tommy nods down at the attendant. "I'll hide with this one in back."

An antsy nod from Alexa. She adjusts her hair and takes a deep breath. Tommy hoists Guzim to his feet and leads him through the door to the storage room.

He closes it, moves his ear to it. He hears the bells attached to the entrance jingle.

"Oh hi," Alexa says in a chipper voice.

The scent of cigar smoke in the store. "Where's Guzim?"

"Are you the man who's supposed to tell me where Dennis is?"

"How about we start by you telling me where Guzim is, sweetheart?"

"He went for coffee."

"And left you in the shop alone?"

"He knew I wouldn't steal anything. You guys can trust me. I was friends with Kreshnik."

"Kreshnik is in the morgue."

"I was ... heartbroken."

A moment. "Still a lot of rumors going around. One of them is that Dennis's girl's brother showed up at that house. That your relation?"

"It ... he ... yes. Unfortunately yes. He came out here looking for me. Totally unprovoked."

"Speaking of relatives, Kreshnik was a second cousin of mine. We Albanians prefer working with family members because we tend to be like-minded. Makes things simpler. Are you and your brother ... like-minded?"

"We couldn't be more different."

"So you're not planning on shooting me?"

"What? Of course not. I'm unarmed. Frisk me if you want."

"Now that's an interesting idea."

"I . . . this has nothing to do with my brother. It's about Dennis. He wants to see me. If you have a way of contacting him, please—"

"You said you dated him. Past tense. So you're single now?"

A moment. "Technically, I guess. I need to talk to—"

"I know you do. And I know where he is. Happy to tell you. I'd be doing a favor for you. Only fair you do one for me."

"What?"

Silence for a few seconds.

"Whoa," she says. "Get your hands off me."

"I thought you wanted me to frisk you."

A nervous laugh from her. "Let's just take it easy."

"I'm trying to take it easy. You're the one being difficult."

"Get your fucking hands off me."

Tommy lets go of Guzim and bursts through the storage-room door. Glimpsing him is Jetmir, an in-shape middle-aged man with black hair slicked back, looks like a retired male porn star. He steps toward Tommy, who shoves him. Jetmir's back whomps the counter, the impact knocking the cigar out of his mouth.

Guzim darts out of the storage area and grasps the scissors from the counter's pencil cup like a knife. He slashes at Tommy, who picks up Jetmir as a shield. The blades slice his shoulder, a red splotch seeping through the white sleeve.

"You Goddamn moron," Jetmir shouts. He elbows Tommy's rib, breaks free from him.

Guzim stabs at Tommy's face. He ducks, then decks his nose, launching him into a printer that tips and thumps the floor, a mess of papers spilling from it. Jetmir punches the back of Tommy's head, knocking him into a stack of cardboard boxes that bursts apart. Jetmir grabs him from behind, his circled arms constricting Tommy's to his sides.

Guzim swipes the scissors. Tommy swings his torso to the side, the blades digging into Jetmir's collar. He screams, stumbles over a trash bin, Tommy wriggling out of his clutch as garbage pours among the paper and cardboard boxes strewn about the floor. Guzim's angry gaze resettles on him.

"Tommy," Alexa says. He looks to her. She tosses an an uncapped pen with a sharp metal tip on the floor. He rushes toward it while Guzim rushes at him. Before the scissors penetrate his head, Tommy picks up the pen and spears the side of Guzim's thigh. His leg buckles.

"This too," Alexa says. She lobs him a ream of paper, five hundred wrapped sheets.

Tommy catches it and smashes an edge into Guzim's head. He drops to a knee, his eyes woozy. Tommy hits him again. He crumples to the floor unconscious.

"Tape up his hands and ankles before he wakes up," Tommy says. Alexa scurries toward a roll of packaging tape.

Bloody Jetmir clenches the strip of metal bells from the door. He smacks it across Tommy's face. A discordant rattle as Tommy backpedals. Jetmir tackles him. Tommy guards his face with his forearms, blocking whacks from the bells.

In his periphery, he spots the loose cigar, its tip still red with heat.

He grips it. And drives the lit end into Jetmir's

chest, cooking a patch of flesh. He yells. Tommy kicks him away, muscles him onto the floor face down, and clasps his hands behind his back.

"Where's Dennis?" Tommy shouts.

"Fuck off."

Tommy tugs Jetmir's hands upward, applying painful pressure to his shoulder blades. "I'll keep going until you give me what I want."

Jetmir grunts. "What's going on here? Aren't you the one dating that FBI agent?"

"Where the fuck is Dennis?"

"Now you're rolling around with his girl, doing shit like this? What's your end game?"

"All we want is his address."

"Why?"

"Doesn't concern you."

"You banging his hoe now?"

"The address."

Jetmir laughs. "Ain't this some juicy shit?"

"You have ten seconds to tell me the address."

"What happened? He pissed her off and you promised to kill him for her?"

"Seven more seconds."

"I'm not telling you shit."

Tommy yanks Jetmir's hands farther upward, his shoulder blades grinding into each other. Jetmir looks toward Alexa and says, "You deserve a lot better than this guido. I know plenty of hot-heads like this. They're unreliable. Treat their women like crap. Do yourself a favor and ditch him."

Tommy flips him around, slugs his mouth. Then again, blood winging out from the edges of his lips. Growling, Jetmir lifts his head, trying to get loose. Tommy punches him again, the back of his skull cracking against the floor, his eyelids closing with unconsciousness. Tommy strikes him again.

"Enough," Alexa shouts.

Tommy punches him once more.

Alexa hugs him from behind. "Stop. Tommy. You're going to kill him. Stop."

Tommy lowers his bloodstained fist.

"Ugh," she says, glancing at the inert gangster. "How's he supposed to tell us where Dennis is now?"

Forty-Two

Katie the concierge sits in a sleek glass room on the Hyacinth's Security floor, around her monitors with high tech readings, in front of her a half-eaten banana split, compliments of the hotel for what she's been through since the bomb-threat call fifty-eight minutes ago.

The resort's billionaire owner, sixty-eight-year-old Colt Dodson, steps to the room's door, a biometric scanner flashing over his eyeball, granting him access. He wears the same Stetson cowboy hat Katie remembers while watching him on TV with her mom back in Minnesota. Somewhat of a pop culture figure after dating an A-list actress for a month in the late 90s, businessman Colt appeared on *Dancing with the Stars* a couple year ago, held on for a few rounds until a botched rumba did him in.

The Director of Security and three of his men greet Colt, who eyes Katie's cleavage for a solid two seconds before introducing himself. He sits beside her.

The concierge line, which Security routed to a speakerphone in the conference room, rings as soon as the sixty-minute mark arrives.

The Director scopes the digits on the caller ID. "It's him."

"All the money I spend on tech and we really can't trace this?" Colt asks.

"Anonymous VoIP number."

Colt groans, then presses a green button on the console. "So why should I give you ten million dollars?"

"Mister Dodson I presume," a voice in a British accent says from the speaker. "If you do not, I would pity whoever is nearby the new addition to your property."

"If you tried to sneak a bomb in here, our tech would've picked it up."

"Please tell your Director of Security, Mister Franklin, to have a look at his email."

Colt turns to the Director, who pulls his phone from his pocket, taps a few buttons with a rushed hand. He shows Colt his screen. Katie peeks at it.

A photo of a bomb from an email address without a sender name, a series of letters and numbers at an obscure domain.

"I kindly ask you to make note of the carpet surrounding the explosive," the voice from the phone says, now German in accent. "As I am sure you know, its distinct light-orange pattern matches that in the Hyacinth's guestrooms. Once you accept that this threat is real, please let me know and we can continue this conversation in a productive fashion."

"You really want to blow up a bunch of innocent people enjoying a vacation?" Colt asks.

"I do not have the power to blow anyone up. Detonation is triggered not by me but a timer. I do have access to an off button. Which I will gladly press if you meet my request. Technically, Mister Dodson, you are the only person who has the power to blow people up. I am merely in a position to save them."

Colt bellylaughs. "That's good. You sound like one of my lawyers. If this whole terrorism thing doesn't work out for you, maybe I can find you a job."

215

"I am not a terrorist, Mister—"

"Yes you are. Speaking of saving people, you're the only person who can save yourself. None of us knows who you are. Shut off the bomb now and you walk off unscathed. But if that thing explodes, a team of feds with an unlimited budget will hunt you the rest of your life."

"I want to shut off the bomb. All I need is my ten—"

"You can't just make a phone call with some voice-scrambler toy, become rich, and get away with it. America doesn't work like that."

"Three thousand two hundred and eleven."

"What?"

"The number of guestrooms at the Hyacinth. A search of all by midnight would make for quite the challenge. Plus create quite the disturbance for your clientele. The casino would clear out. Revenue would come to a standstill. The customer base might not return for weeks. Ready for the Bitcoin instructions?"

Colt grinds his teeth. "I need to discuss this with my team."

"All those suckers sitting at your slot machines believe in luck. But, as a casino proprietor, I suspect you do not. Finding and disabling the device in time would require an extreme amount of luck. Or end this problem practically, and quietly, with a simple payment."

"I'll . . . call you back."

"I will be waiting. But not for long." A moment. "Loved you on *Dancing with the Stars* by the way."

The terrorist hangs up.

# FORTY-THREE

Tommy and Alexa, in the shadowy back room of the shipping shop, peer down at the two Albanian gangsters tied with packaging tape. Jetmir is still motionless, eyes closed, lines of blood running from his mouth, while Guzim has awoken from his paper ream-induced daze.

"He's going to die if you don't bring him to a hospital," Guzim says. "He has cancer."

"Bullshit," Tommy says.

"Lung cancer. After a beating like that, he can't just lie there without a doctor checking him out."

"What's he doing huffing stogies if he's got lung cancer?"

"Told me smoking got more enjoyable after the diagnosis. I don't know."

Tommy paces among the store supplies. He says

to Alexa, "We could wait here for him to wake up, then keep pressing him for Dennis's address."

"Or we wait . . . and he never wakes up. Making you guilty of manslaughter. And me an accessory."

He runs a hand through his hair. "You really believe that cancer story?"

"No. But cancer or not, he definitely needs medical attention. Besides, even if he woke up, you really think he's going to give you the address after that number you did on his face?"

Tommy is silent for a while. Then kicks a shelf. "Fine. We'll bring him to the Goddam hospital."

"I'll get my car." She scurries out the door.

"What about me?" Guzim asks. "I need to see a doctor too. I got stabbed in the leg."

"You'll be fine here for a while." Tommy leans his back against a metal beam, secures him to it with tape. "After I find Dennis, I'll make an anonymous nine-one-one call, send a cop here to cut you loose."

"What do I do until then?"

Tommy sticks a tape strip over his mouth. "Ponder a career change."

Among Guzim's mumbling, Tommy hoists out-cold Jetmir over his shoulder, then carries him out the front door.

Night has fallen, the headlights of Alexa's Camaro shining through a foggy blackness. Tommy sticks his head outside, confirms no onlookers around, then loads Jetmir into her backseat.

He sits beside her. She hits the gas. They exit the strip-mall lot and ride a North Vegas road through the neglected neighborhood. The car is hushed besides the hum of the engine and wispy breathing from the backseat.

In about fifteen minutes the red sign of St. Margaret's Hospital glows on the horizon. Alexa motors up to the entrance and idles. Tommy exits the car, hauls bloody-faced Jetmir out, and lays him on the pavement. A woman pushing a man in a wheelchair gapes.

Tommy climbs back into his seat. Alexa zooms away from the hospital. In the rearview mirror, Tommy sees the image of Jetmir decreasing in size. Alexa turns. The image disappears, along with their only realistic chance to learn Dennis's location.

# FORTY-FOUR

Tommy's head still throbs from the brawl at the shipping shop. He puts his hand over the vent in Alexa's car, the air warm despite the dial cranked to cool.

"I need to get that fixed," she says.

He leans back in his seat.

"Instead of pretending I had engine trouble," she says, "maybe I should've had Guzim check out my AC." She looks at him as if waiting for a response to her joke.

Not in the mood for jokes, he doesn't give her a reaction. Quiet for a while.

"I'm glad we dropped the other one off at the hospital," she says. "Wouldn't have forgiven ourselves if he didn't make it."

"Maybe he didn't deserve to make it. Guy like that

was probably into all kinds of despicable shit."

"Possibly. Sure. But I still think we made the right decision." A pause. "Didn't we?"

"I don't know. What I do know is we're screwed."

"If Dennis really wants me with him, you said he'll send someone to look for me, right? Maybe we can get information off that person."

He peeks at her in profile. "It's a longshot. Not to mention, waiting for them to attack us puts us at a disadvantage. No element of surprise on our side. We'll need a gun."

"All right. We'll get a gun."

He clenches his jaw. "It's my fault we're in this position. My fucking fault."

"What do you mean?"

He punches the glovebox, a strong thud.

"Chill out," she says. "You didn't do anything wrong."

"I was close. I was so close. That asshole knew where Dennis was." Tommy points at the side of his head. "Had an address in his brain. All he had to do was say it. He was right in front of me. Right in front of me. And instead of using tact, I beat the crap out of him. To the point where he couldn't even open his mouth and give me what I needed."

"Hey . . . it was . . . you know, stressful back there. You lost your cool. I . . . I get it."

He wipes some sweat from his cheek with his forearm. "Maybe it's true what he said. Maybe I am some hot-head. Maybe you should do what he told you and ditch me."

"No way. We're a team now."

He stares out the window, his fist on his lips. "Big difference between me and Buckles, I'll tell you that."

A moment. "Buckles the dog? My family dog?"

"Nothing."

He dips his chin, closes his eyes. A bob of his head as the car merges into another lane. They don't talk for about a minute.

"Hey," she says. "Before we get the gun, I want to eat something."

He opens his eyes.

"I didn't have any pizza before," she says. Then points at a *CVS* sign, visible through the fog about a half-mile up the road.

"You want to eat at CVS?"

"I love CVS." She smiles.

Her smile makes him feel a little better.

She pulls into the parking lot, exits the Camaro, and walks through the convenience store entrance like a little girl walking into Disneyworld. She grabs a red shopping basket and looks at the rows of products framed by white walls and bright lights.

He steps to her side, hands in his pockets. "I don't get it. What're you so juiced up about?"

"It's all the little stuff you need. In one place."

"Yeah. I know. Everyone does. It's CVS."

"They're new to me. First time I set foot in one was when I moved out here." She walks toward the refrigerated section. "We didn't have one in Willince. We didn't have much of anything. Most of my stuff I ordered online. If I needed something like that day, I'd have to drive two towns over. They had a drugstore, but small. Nothing like one of these babies." She opens a fridge, puts a bottle of water in her basket.

"Your brother . . . he definitely has a rural vibe to him. Guess I'd believe he was never in a CVS. But you . . . you come off different. Nothing like him or your mom."

They veer into another aisle. Eyeballing an assortment of nuts, she says, "I tried to help her. When I got old enough to realize things weren't right with her. Even though she's been envious of me since I was a kid. For something . . . something completely fucked up and out of my control. Still, I tried giving her my help." She drops a pack of almonds into her basket. "But she didn't want it. And my brother . . . she has him so under her thumb, she turned him on me. And now I don't speak to either of them."

"Kurt's in a hospital. For you. I'd give him another chance. He's a good kid."

She takes a deep breath. "You want anything while we're here?"

"I'm okay."

She adds a Twix to her basket, then pays. He trails her to the Camaro. They get in.

She tosses her plastic bag in the backseat. "Thanks for looking out for me."

"It's nothing."

"What you went through fighting both those guys . . . that wasn't nothing. You could've been home in San Diego by now."

"Ah. I'm alive because of your brother. I owed him one."

"So that's the only reason you're looking out for me? My brother?"

He gazes into her eyes. "No. Wouldn't want to see anything bad happen to you."

She moves over to his seat. And straddles him. "How about this? Is this bad?"

A moment. "No. That's not bad."

"How about this?" She peels off her *Viva Las Vegas* tee shirt, revealing the black bra he saw before. "Is this bad?"

"No. That's not bad."

She grabs his right hand. Puts it on her left breast. "How about this? This bad?"

No sound in the car but their breathing. He moves his hand to her face, pulls her toward him. They start kissing.

# FORTY-FIVE

Albanian music radiates from the speaker on Cameroon Joe's iPhone, propped up on a shelf in the storage room of the Shooting Star Pawnshop, the money washing business where Dennis has been hiding. No windows, clusters of second-hand items on the floor and shelves, ranging from home appliances to collectible coins to retro arcade machines.

Cameroon Joe and Troka pass back and forth a bottle of raki while Dennis sits on a folding chair in the corner, watching the sand cascade through an hourglass he grabbed from the inventory.

He recalls recess one afternoon in third grade. A classmate, Lindsay Maggen, skinned her knee playing boxball. The sight of the blood scared him. He sprinted to the teacher for help. Now, because of him, a bomb may do a lot more to people than skin their knees.

"You had to hear my lawyer on the phone," Troka

says to Cameroon Joe. "He really played that cowboy hat-wearing Hyacinth prick. Shouldn't be long till he pays up. Dennis Notch, the man with the golden tongue."

"Silver," Cameroon Joe says. He swigs from the raki bottle and hands it to Troka.

"What?"

"Silver tongue. That's the expression. A man with a silver tongue."

"Gold is better than silver. More expensive."

"I know. But that's not the expression."

"Well, I'm making it an expression."

"You can't just make an expression."

"Of course you can. Where do you think the silver one came from? At some point, somebody just made it up."

A pensive tilt to Cameroon Joe's head, the lighting striping his sunglass lenses. "If you're doing a new one, go even better than gold. Platinum. A man with a platinum tongue."

"Rhodium is more expensive than platinum."

"A man with a rhodium tongue." Cameroon Joe shakes his head. "I don't like it. Sounds too clinical. Like a medical condition."

"Mmm." Troka says to Dennis, "Have a drink with us. It'll be good luck while we wait for the callback."

"I do not believe a depressant in my system would make for a net positive right now."

Troka walks to Dennis, stepping around a crate of old action figures, the pawnshop logo on the side. He sets a hand on his shoulder. "Get your head straight, son. We need you to see this thing to the finish line."

"I will."

Troka's phone rings. "Yeah?" he says into it. Ten seconds or so pass. His cheery demeanor disintegrates.

"Is that right?"

Dennis and Cameroon Joe huddle around him.

"I see," Troka says into the phone. "All right. Thanks. Get well soon." He hangs up.

"Who was that?" Cameroon Joe asks.

"Jetmir."

"He all right?"

"He just woke up in the hospital. Said Thomas Dapino kicked the crap out of him." Troka nods at Dennis. "He's looking for you. And he's apparently with your girlfriend."

"Alexa?"

"He didn't mention a name."

Dennis opens an untraceable voice-over-IP app on his burner phone, dials Alexa's number, committed to memory.

"Are you seriously calling her?" Troka asks.

"She could be in trouble."

"What I tell you? Hang up."

Dennis turns his back to the Albanians.

"Hello?" Alexa says.

"Honey. Is everything okay?"

"Dennis?"

"Yes love."

Silence from her. But he detects another voice in the background, male, too distant to make out what it's saying.

"Who are you with?" Dennis asks.

"I'm ... uh ... where are you?"

Dennis peeks over his shoulder at the irate-looking Albanians. "I am not at liberty to provide my whereabouts over the phone. Are you with Thomas Dapino?"

A pause. "Who?"

"I ... heard something. Let's talk in person. I need

to see you. Are you still mad at me about our little misunderstanding at the townhouse?"

A moment. "I really want to see you too. Just tell me where you are. I'll come now."

"I . . . I can't do that."

Cameroon Joe tears the phone out of Dennis's hand and ends the call. Then slaps his face and shouts, "Who do you think you are?"

Dennis recenters his head after the hit, its sting still on his cheek. "I need you to bring her to me."

Cameroon Joe laughs. "Fuck off, lawyer."

"After we have the Hyacinth money," Troka says. "That was our agreement."

"Things changed since our agreement. If she's with Dapino, he could be threatening her. Trying to leverage her to get to me. He seems to be good at this sort of thing. Got to me at my house before the cops or feds. We need to pry her away from him. Not just for my good. All of ours. Do you two want him finding me before the Hyacinth deal is done?"

Troka folds his arms, blows out a big puff of air. "Mmm. Do you even know where they are?"

"When Alexa was working guys at casinos, I feared for her safety. So took certain precautions. That she is unaware of. They may be of use for this endeavor." He turns to Cameroon Joe. "When you reach them, she will resist leaving with you. If you have to induce her cooperation in some way, I understand. But if you hurt her, I will bite the nose off your face."

"This Dapino guy just put Jetmir in the hospital," Troka says. "Seems like he'll be putting up a fight himself."

"You bet your ass he will. The only way to stop him is to kill him." He bites his lip for a second. "Let's make sure we do that."

# FORTY-SIX

Alexa drives herself and Tommy toward a ghetto, a touch of sweat still on their foreheads from the sex in the CVS parking lot. It was good. Twice.

They took about ten minutes to collect their ripped-off clothing from the nooks of the car, her panties still missing, nothing on beneath her jean shorts.

"Have you bought a gun off the street before?" she asks.

"No."

"You know what to do?"

"Drug dealers post up on corners. They're easy to spot. We pull up to one of them. Ask if he can get us a piece. From there, it'll be a price negotiation just like buying anything else."

"I'm kinda excited."

He grins. "Let me make the actual exchange though. If we happen to approach an undercover cop, I don't want you going down for it. Not with that blackmail case hanging over you."

She sighs. "Almost forgot about that for a minute."

"I think you should forget about it permanently. Make money some other way."

"We going to continue our debate from the bowling alley?"

"No. No. I don't want to debate you on whether or not what you did was justified. I just think you'd get more out of a different line of work."

"What kind of work?"

"I'm unemployed. Clearly no expert myself. I don't have an answer for you. You're good at tricking people. And you're pretty as hell. I suppose that's a solid combo for what you do. But you've got more to offer."

A moment. "Like go back to waitressing?"

"You're decisive. Don't scare easily. Can read people. You can do a lot more than waitress. Just keep your mind open. You'll figure it out."

She lets out a long exhale. Then grabs her pink-cased phone from the cupholder. "Time for some music." She enters her passcode, *0125*.

"Birthday January twenty-fifth?"

"Yes, my PIN is my bday. Guess I'm a basic bitch." He chuckles. She taps some buttons, streams "Paris, Texas" by Tim Hill. She hums along, says, "Wish I had a decent singing voice."

"I don't have one either. Tried once in our sixth-grade talent show. Me and my buddy Josh somehow thought it would be cool to belt out 'Who Let the Dogs Out.' I was so bad I'm pretty sure I got suspended."

She laughs. "Does this happen to be on video?"

"No comment."

In a few minutes, the scenery outside decays. Graffiti, barred-window storefronts, littered sidewalks.

She makes a right. In the rearview mirror, he notices the headlights of an SUV making the same turn. "Huh," he says.

"What?"

"That car's been behind us."

She glimpses the mirror. "You've been paying attention to a car behind us?"

"Of course."

"You think they're following us?"

"I don't know." He nods at a green traffic light a few hundred feet away. "Slow down. Catch this next red. I'll try to get a look at the driver."

An anxious breath from her. She eases off the gas, the Camaro dropping to about twenty-five miles per hour. The light turns yellow. She coasts to a stop as it turns red.

Tommy spins around, pretending to look for something in the backseat. His gaze tilts to the rear window, outside it a haze of Camaro exhaust tinted red by its brake lights. Beyond that a silver Mercedes G-Wagon. Its driver a thirty-something male in sunglasses.

"You recognize him?" she asks, glimpsing the rearview.

"No."

"He sort of seems Albanian, right?"

"Look, try to stay calm. Then we—"

She slams the gas, racing through the red light.

"Holy shit," Tommy says. "What're you doing?"

The G-Wagon's engine roars. It zooms through the red light too, cutting off a honking sedan.

"I was right," Alexa blurts. "He's coming after us."

Tommy's eyes bounce between her and their pursuer. The Camaro accelerates to about fifty. She hooks a screeching left onto a quiet road checkered with closed shops.

A moment later, the G-Wagon does too, its powerful high beams slicing the fog.

"Pull over," Tommy says, squinting in the lights' glare.

"You kidding?"

"Let me confront him."

"What? No."

"He's by himself. I can handle this."

"It's too . . . no. Okay? No. Not without a gun. We need one. You said it yourself. I don't want to see you get hurt." Her panicky foot presses down on the gas. The G-Wagon speeds up, about ten feet off her tail.

"I'll take my chances. Pull—"

*Prudoom*, a loud noise echoes. The Camaro hitches. Tommy notices the gangster leaning out his window with a pistol.

"Did he just shoot out my fucking tire?" she asks.

"Stay calm."

She peeks at her rearview. And ducks.

"Keep your eyes on the road," Tommy says.

"I don't want to get my Goddamn brains blown out."

The Camaro swerves. Tommy unbuckles his seatbelt, leans over, and clasps the wheel, attempting to steady the car. It whips left. Then right. Then a lot to the left. Crosses into the next lane, bashes into a curb, then a mailbox, then a streetlamp. It flips.

The top skids against the sidewalk, sparks, glass spraying upside-down Tommy and Alexa. Still belted, she remains in her seat while Tommy bangs around the interior. His head nails the gearshift.

*Dudank*. The car slams into a building, stops moving.

Shards of glass mixed into Alexa's hair. She seems fazed, but okay, just a little blood on her elbow. Her underwear turned up, a ball of pink fabric resting on the Camaro's ceiling beside her similar-toned phone.

Leather loafers appear on the sidewalk. The handsome man they belong to bends down, peers into the car through his sunglasses. His arm juts inside. He undoes Alexa's seatbelt, then grasps her forearm, starts yanking her through the shattered window.

"Alexa," Tommy says, grabbing her ankle.

Smirking, the gangster points his pistol at Tommy.

A bang fills the overturned Camaro as Tommy dives toward the backseat out of the bullet's path, his grip breaking off Alexa's ankle.

The gangster drags her through the driver window, her body contorting to avoid the jagged rim of glass.

Tommy opens a backdoor, takes cover on the other side of the Camaro near the front. Something wet on his check. He wipes it with his Lucky Larry's shirt. Crimson. Blood. He feels more welling inside his ear, not from the flesh, deeper down. Dizziness too. Internal bleeding. Must be from his head smashing into the gearshift.

Alexa's shrieking masks the sound of any footsteps, Tommy unsure which way the gangster may be approaching.

*Pladoom*. The rearview mirror inches from Tommy's head explodes.

He crawls to the nose of the vehicle. The sound of police sirens rings in the distance.

He peeks around the car, notices the gangster running toward his G-Wagon clasping Alexa, her feet flailing a few inches off the pavement. Tommy rushes to the knocked-over mailbox and heaves it off the ground. Holding the hundred-plus-pound object in front of his face and torso as a shield, he chases them.

A vibration and clang as a bullet strikes the mailbox. He charges in the direction of the G-Wagon without visibility of it. The police sirens louden.

An engine starts. He lets go of the mailbox, the silhouettes of Alexa and the gangster inside the G-Wagon. He leaps onto its back, grasping for the roof rack bars.

Just before he clutches one, the car accelerates forward, splitting from Tommy. He plummets to the ground. Catching his breath, he stares at a graffitied building wall, on it a spray-painted playing card like a jack but instead of a man at its center, a skeleton.

Spinning blue and red lights illuminate the wall. The cops are here.

But Alexa is gone.

# FORTY-SEVEN

Alexa rides in the backseat of the G-Wagon with zip ties around her wrists and ankles, the driver bobbing his head to the Bee Gees' "Night Fever" on the stereo.

He pulls into the parking lot of a one-story business, a *Shooting Star Pawnshop* sign elevated over the roof. No lights on, it appears closed. He parks in back, one other vehicle there, and steps out.

He tosses her over his shoulder like a rug and knocks on the business's rear door. It opens.

Dennis.

He smiles at her, burns stretching and bending across the left half of his face. He looks like a monster in a low-budget horror movie.

"Hey babe," he says.

She says nothing for a few seconds. Then a winded

"Hi."

He steps to the side. The gangster carries her into a storage area.

An older, stumpy man waits there. He eyes her. "You were right. She is a looker."

The gangster sets her down on a folding chair. Dennis places his hands on her thighs. She wonders how they found her all the way out in the ghetto.

"Let's consider this a fresh start," Dennis says. "Soon we will begin a life together in a new home."

A chill overtakes her skin at this thought. But she does not rebuke him. Not tied up, not with that deranged gleam in his eyes, not with these two other men, both Albanian gangsters she assumes, at his flanks.

"You sure you want to marry this chick?" the driver asks with a snicker.

"I don't need relationship advice from you. Now can I please return to the conversation I was having with my girlfriend?"

"She might be someone else's girlfriend by now."

"What do you mean?"

"That dude she was with. Dapino. Good-looking guy. In good shape too. I get the appeal."

"He was trying to use her to get to me, idiot. They are not dating."

"Didn't seem like that to me."

"Maybe if you spent more energy on killing him, like you were supposed to, instead of trying to infer his romantic thoughts, he wouldn't still be out there, and we wouldn't still have a problem."

"I didn't have to infer anything. Saw it."

"Saw what?"

Cameroon Joe smirks. "Her underwear."

"Is this some perverted joke? If so, I'm going to—"

"Not a joke. When I went into her car. Little pink panties. Balled up." He shrugs. "Now, is it possible she took them off because she was warm, wanted to remove a layer of clothing to cool down? Maybe. But . . . maybe not."

"Is this accurate?" Dennis asks her.

"Of course not. Look at the grin on this bozo's face. He's messing with you. Getting some sick enjoyment out of making you jealous."

Dennis sinks to his knees. His long fingers drift to her jean shorts. He undoes their button.

"Den, what're you doing?" she asks, pushing him away with her bound hands.

He bats them to the side, unzips her fly. Looks between her legs. Underwear missing.

His left eyelids twitch. He lowers his head into her lap. She looks away, feels the coarseness of his burnt hair on her for about half a minute.

He grasps an hourglass and hurls it against the wall, an eruption of sand.

Quiet for a while.

"I get why you're pissed," the older gangster says. "But we must stay focused. If this Dapino fellow was schtupping your girl, he's going to want to find her. Gives him more of a reason to come at us. We need to stop him. Where is he?"

The driver says, "The cops were seconds away from him when I left. He could be with them. Going directly at him at this point is a bad strategy."

"You had a chance to shoot him and blew it. Fixing this is on you."

"There's a way I can trip him up without going near him or the police."

"What is it?"

# FORTY-EIGHT

Tommy sits on a curb watching a tow truck driver clamp chains to Alexa's Camaro. Four cops stand by the wreck trading theories, excitement in their voices since they realized this isn't just a car accident, but a link to the high-profile Dennis Notch manhunt.

One of the officers, a chunky patrolman about thirty named Chester, saunters to Tommy, asks, "How you feeling, Dapino?"

"You guys have any idea who the G-Wagon belongs to?"

"Metro has a file on the Albanian mob. A few affiliated vehicles in there. Unfortunately no Mercedes G-Wagons. But we've got an APB out for it. Going to fire up the chopper for an overheard search too. It's a pretty unique car. I'm optimistic."

"I'm not. This is Vegas. A lot of flashy cars. A lot of

roads. A lot of parking lots. And these guys are smart."

A heavy breath from Chester. "I wish we had a better plan. But Metro's file on the Albanians is light. From what my captain says, the feds may know more than us, but still, not a ton. We're all . . . doing the best we can. Why do you give a damn about this girl, anyway? She's a scam artist."

"No she's not."

"According to the FBI, she—"

"Technically the FBI is right. But it's not who she is."

Chester assesses Tommy's eyes. "You and her . . . you two . . . you weren't . . . you know?"

"Look, I care about her. That's all you need to know. And if someone I care about is in trouble, I'll put my head through fucking walls to get them out of it."

Chester nods a couple times. Then scopes the area, cracked windows on abandoned buildings, shadowy alleys, a roving junkie. "How the hell do you imagine Dennis and the Albanians knew to look for Alexa all the way out here?"

"I've been asking myself the same question." Tommy points at a cardboard box on the sidewalk, in it various personal items of his and Alexa's the tow truck driver retrieved from the car, her pink-cased phone among them. "She told me Dennis bought her a phone as a gift."

"So?"

"Possessive guy with a dark mind dating an attractive girl. I bet he installed some location-tracking app on it before he gave it to her."

"Huh. Sounds about right." Chester sits on the curb beside Tommy, his knees cracking. He pats his gut. "I've got to get in better shape, Dapino. But insulin resistance. It's holding me back."

"Yeah. That'll get you."

"So, looks like I'm heading out of here. Captain wants me to cruise around hawk-eyeing for G-Wagons. Since you saw the driver's face, nobody better to ID him than you. Want to ride shotgun with me?"

If he rode with Chester, he could react alongside him to any leads flowing in over police radio, while if he pursued Dennis and the Albanians solo, that intel would be inaccessible. But, in the presence of a cop, an illegal gun would be out. If Tommy comes across the criminals, he would be forced to face them unarmed.

He thinks about this for a couple seconds. Then extends his hand. "Yeah, let's rock."

Chester shakes it. Then loads the cardboard box of personal items onto his car's backseat. He and Tommy cruise around North Vegas for about an hour without luck, then loop toward the Strip.

Tommy gazes out the window at the flocks of pedestrians on the sidewalks, neon signs burning through the fog high above them, *Aria, Planet Hollywood, Caesars Palace.* The colors seep together in Tommy's field of vision. It's blurred since the car accident, must be a symptom of the internal bleeding in his head.

If Chester discerns the condition, he'll pester Tommy about going to a hospital. Tommy lifts his index finger to his left ear, pretends to scratch it while dabbing blood pooled inside.

"I got to ask you something," Chester says, pointing at Tommy's Lucky Larry's shirt.

"Shoot."

"The casino. When Metro had the helicopter out for you before. Apparently you walked in . . . but never walked out. What really happened? How'd you pull that off? I'm curious."

"Some tricks I've got to keep to myself."

"Maybe I can bribe you." Chester reaches into the glovebox and pulls out a glass bottle of reddish sauce, on it a label that looks like it was made from a nametag, *Chester's Choice* scrawled on it in marker. He hands it to Tommy.

"What do we have here?"

"Nine years of labor. And love. That's what we have there. Took me that long to perfect the recipe. Just a month away from getting it in a local grocery store. Best damn barbecue sauce you'll ever taste."

Tommy shakes the bottle. "I like the color. The texture too. Seems ... substantial."

"It's a meal in and of itself. Don't even need any meat." A pause. "But of course ... you're going to want to put it on some meat."

"Of course."

"Here's my proposal. After we find Alexa, after we arrest Dennis Notch, we're stopping for some brisket to celebrate. I know a great twenty-four-hour buffet. And you're going to taste that BBQ sauce. And you're going to love it. And I'll let you keep that advanced-release bottle. But in exchange, you've got to tell me how you pulled off the Lucky Larry's move."

"Let's say nobody got hurt during this move. But not all of it was fully legal. Could I tell you and not worry about you cuffing me?"

"Nobody got hurt, not even a little?"

"Nobody got hurt."

"You're on."

"I think we're going to make a good duo, Chester." Tommy sets the bottle in the cardboard box of his and Alexa's belongings in the backseat. "So how you going to find the time to launch a barbecue sauce empire when you're patrolling the streets of Las Vegas?"

"My wife, Gwen, she's got my back." Chester reaches under his sizable ass and pulls his wallet from his pocket. He flips it open to a photo of him and a full-figured blond woman holding hoagies with Chester's Choice drizzled atop. "We're a duo too."

"She's helping you with the sauce?"

"I'm in charge of making the stuff, which I can do in my garage after my shifts. She's in charge of the marketing and distribution. And you've got to see her. She's great with all that. Used to manage a big department store."

Tommy gazes at their faces in the photo. "You look good together. You look happy." He focuses on the picture for another moment, then passes the wallet to grinning Chester.

A male voice says from the police radio, "Ten fifty-six, Diamond Plaza, Paradise. Female, early twenties."

Chester doesn't answer the call, continuing along the Strip. "Eh, let someone else get it. We've got a G-Wagon to find."

He and Tommy cruise side streets for about twenty minutes. No G-Wagons.

The voice returns to the police radio, says, "Possible ID on Diamond Plaza ten fifty-six. Alexa Thoss."

Chester's eyes widen. He snatches the handset from its stand, says into it, "Five twenty-four, copy." He hits a switch on his dashboard, the siren activating. Then makes a U-turn.

"What the hell is going on?" Tommy asks.

Chester eyes him for a moment, then looks ahead.

"Dispatch," Tommy blurts. "What they say about Alexa?"

"Nothing definitive. It was just a report. That's all."

"A report about what?"

"No need to worry about anything. Not yet. We'll go to Diamond Plaza. See what's really happening."

"The guy mentioned a code ten fifty-six. What's that mean?"

"You're . . . making me jumpy. I can't do my job if I'm jumpy."

"Chester, it's a simple question. What's a ten fifty-six?"

He does not answer. Vehicles make awkward turns to get to the edges of Las Vegas Boulevard and clear a path for the cop car. Chester weaves through the scattered gaps.

He drives into Paradise, an unincorporated town next to Las Vegas that houses many of the hotels and casinos associated with Sin City. He approaches a mall, an arced *Diamond Plaza* sign in front of it.

A pair of police cars near the mall's eight-story parking structure, their lights spinning onto two dozen or so observers bordering yellow *Do Not Cross* tape.

Chester veers toward the scene, more details surfacing. An ambulance with its backdoors open. Two cops on crowd control. A tall man in a black windbreaker, across the back in white letters, *Coroner*.

Chester parks. Tommy exits the car a second before him. Through spaces between onlookers' heads and shoulders, Tommy notices two EMTs pushing a stretcher toward the ambulance. A body bag on top, the outline of a human being beneath it. About Alexa's height.

Tommy is still for a few seconds. Then turns to Chester and asks in a deflated voice, "Can you tell me what a ten fifty-six is now?"

Chester emits a lengthy exhale. "Suicide."

# FORTY-NINE

Tommy paces just outside the yellow police tape at the mall. He watches Chester and two other Metro PD officers on the other side, a buxom Black woman around forty and a spray-tanned man about thirty-five, the sleeves of his police shirt tailored up a nudge to showcase his built biceps.

The dead body now whisked away, the spectators have dispersed, a hush to the parking lot besides the chatter of the three cops.

Tommy, stepping over the police tape, says, "I still don't see why everyone's so positive that was Alexa."

A ticked-off slant to the muscular cop's jaw. He turns to Chester. "Remind me why you brought a civilian here again? And remind me why he thinks he has the right to interrupt me while I'm doing policework?"

"He's in the business," Chester says. "Well, sort of.

A PI. Well, an unemployed PI. Just trying to help. Fill him in."

The cop spits on the asphalt. "We found a note. A suicide note." He points at the top of the eight-story parking structure. "Up there. Right by where she jumped. Signed by Alexa Thoss. Convincing enough?"

Chester, with a diplomatic grin, saunters to Tommy and whispers, "Why don't you wait on the other side of the tape?"

Tommy peeks over Chester's shoulder, asks the other cop, "You get a look at the face?"

The female officer shakes her head. "Honey, no such thing to see." She holds out her left palm. Then smacks it with her right. "Splat. Baby girl hit the pavement facedown from all the way up in the sky. Nothing but a mess where a face once was."

"So you couldn't officially ID her?"

"We pulled up Alexa Thoss's social media. The jumper was blond, just like her. Same height, five four, just like her. From the look of the hands, seemed about the same age, twenty-one. Same skinny little figure with some titties too."

Chester says to Tommy, "I know you were trying to keep her safe. But this is Vegas. Crazy crap like this happens all the time. Sounds like this young woman had a hell of a day. A hell of a life. And the stress . . . got the best of her."

"Bullshit. She did have a hard day. And a hard life. But I was with her just before. She wasn't suicidal then. What changed in such a short timeframe?"

"I . . . Dapino, I'm just a beat cop. I'm no shrink. I'm sure you'll get that answer eventually. But we don't have it for you now."

"Surveillance. From the parking structure. There's got to be footage."

Chester gazes at the two other officers as if requesting a response.

"The mall people are working on getting us the tape," the man says.

"Make them work faster," Tommy says.

"That's enough from you. Get the hell out of my face before I throw you in the back of my car. Chester, I swear to God with this fucking guy."

Clutching Tommy's arm, Chester guides him under the police tape. And out across the asphalt. "Wait here."

Tommy removes Chester's hand from his arm. And walks in circles, his dizziness worsening.

# FIFTY

Dennis locks himself inside the pawnshop's bathroom and flips on the sink, the noise drowning out the sound of his hyperventilating.

He imagines the beautiful thing he and Alexa once had. Before she screwed that son of a bitch Dapino and tarnished it. He throws some water on his face. It stings his wounds. Lights off, he gazes at his muted reflection in the shadowed mirror. A man alone in a tight, dark space with a slight foul odor.

Since his release from prison, he's avoided contact with his old life, including his mom and dad. But now, for whatever reason, he needs to hear their voices.

He shuts off the sink. With his burner, he dials the landline number of his parents' home in well-to-do Poolesville, Maryland. While it rings, he sits on the closed toilet, feet up, thighs against his chest.

"Hello?" his mom says.

"Hi. It's me."

A moment. "Dennis?"

"Yeah."

Another moment. "Oh my. Dennis. I can't believe ... it's ... it's so good to hear from you."

"Are you following the local news out here?"

"Umm ... out where, exactly? Honey, we don't even know where you're living these days."

"Nevada. Las Vegas."

"What's on the news in Las Vegas?"

"Never ... never mind."

"Ehh. Okay." A long pause. "So ... how are you? What have you been up to?"

He fiddles with his shoelace. "I don't know. Just working."

"You found a job out there? You like it?"

"I'm more an ... entrepreneur."

"Your own business. Great. I'm so happy for you. Ever since you were a little boy, you had perseverance and smarts. That's all it takes to get anywhere in life." His dad's voice in the background. "It's Dennis," his mom says with cheer.

About ten seconds later his dad comes on the line. "Vegas, huh? Your mother and I will come out and visit. Just tell us when."

"I don't know ... I'm not sure how long I'll be staying here."

"Oh. Okay, all right. Where to next? We'll visit you there."

"Not sure."

"Right. Okay. But your mother ... she just mentioned some business out there. It's the type of outfit you can pick up and move? Just like that?"

"As long as I have a phone and a computer, I can

work from wherever."

"You were always good with technology. Remember when I got my first cellphone?"

"Yeah, I remember."

"I paid all this money for it and here I am thinking the damn thing was broke. I was two seconds away from flinging it out the window before you helped me."

"I just told you to hit the send button."

"Which was crucial. With regular phones, the kind I had my whole life, you dial the number and voila, call goes through. With these new gadgets, they sneak in an extra step without making a big announcement about it. You were so young, but you figured it out. One look. 'Dad, no, you have to hit this.' Your brother laughed at me. Oh, remember how he laughed that night at the dinner table?"

"Yeah, Dad. I do. I do."

"Hold on. Someone else wants to say hi to you. One second."

In a bit, a bark over the phone, his parents' Golden Retriever.

"You hear Oslo say hi?" his dad asks.

Dennis grins. "Yeah. I heard him."

"Casino industry, huh? I can see it Dennis. You may not have a law license anymore, but those skills of yours can translate into most lines of work. Negotiating. That's your ticket. You've got it. And businesses need it. So what is it you're selling to the casinos? Dice and roulette wheels and all that jazz? Or do you deal with the restaurants and lounges?"

"It's . . . it's complicated. Maybe I'll explain it another time."

"All right. Well, don't give up. Never give up. Glad I instilled that in you and your brother. I always knew you'd land on your feet after . . . after, eh . . . well, after everything."

"Thanks, Dad."

"Call me if you need anything. I'm proud of you. Bye, Son."

A tear rolls down Dennis's cheek. "Bye."

He hangs up, dips his head between his knees, his arms dangling at his sides. He stays in this position for a while. Until the phone rings. An incoming call via his voice-over-IP app, "Hyacinth Hotel & Casino" on the screen.

He clears his throat, activates his voice concealer, and answers. "Have you come to your senses?"

"Yes," Colt Dodson says.

"Good."

"Not for you."

"Excuse me?"

"I decided you're not getting any of my money."

A pause. "Then blood will be on your hands. I sent you photographic proof of—"

"Photos could be doctored. Ninety-nine percent of bomb threats are bogus. I've thought about it and have no reason to believe yours is any different. Don't call me again." He hangs up.

Dennis stares down at the toilet seat. He can't tell the Albanians about this. Without a potential monetary gain, they'll have no reason to keep harboring a fugitive. He must string them along from now until midnight, arranging on the sly a new way out of the country.

A knock on the door. "What the hell is going on in there?" Cameroon Joe asks. "You taking a long shit or jerking off?"

"Coming out now."

"Who were you talking to?"

"What?"

"When I was walking over, I swore I heard you talking."

Dennis opens the door. "You must be hearing things."

Cameroon Joe peers at him with skepticism.

# FIFTY-ONE

Chester's tall, rotund frame approaches Tommy in the mall parking lot.

"You see the surveillance footage?" Tommy asks.

Chester nods. "We've got it from here."

"Well, what the hell was on it?"

Chester dabs sweat on his forehead with the back of his hand. "Take an Uber back to your motel. Get some rest, Dapino. You need it."

"I'll only need more of it if you don't tell me what was on that tape."

"Nothing was on the tape."

"What?"

"The amount of security cameras in parking structures is typically very low considering their surface area. With all the columns and cars, field of view is limited, so most businesses only invest in cameras at the entrances and exits. We did notice a young blonde walking in. But nothing captured the jump."

"The blonde's face . . . Alexa's?"

"Older camera. The footage was grainy. Too hard to tell."

Tommy thinks for a moment. "Criminals are known to do meetups in parking structures."

"Yep. Because of what I said, the low camera count."

"Don't you find that a bit of a coincidence?"

"Why, because Alexa was a criminal?"

"No. Because she was kidnapped by criminals. Then not long after, she apparently kills herself in a place criminals know won't capture anything on surveillance."

"You suggesting this wasn't a suicide . . . but a murder?"

A pause. "I don't know." A cold streak runs through Tommy's gut. Suicide or murder, either way Alexa is dead.

"So they track her down in North Vegas. A guy with a gun gets hold of her. But doesn't try to shoot her. Instead tries to shoot you. If he wanted her gone, why not just pull the trigger then? Why go through the trouble of chucking her off the top of a parking structure?"

"I . . . you're right. I have no answer." Tommy leans against the post of a stop sign. "But something still doesn't add up about this whole thing."

"You're drained. You need sleep. Get—"

"I'm not giving up on her."

# FIFTY-TWO

On the pawnshop floor, Alexa cries for the dead hooker. Dennis is conversing with the two gangsters by a Skee-Ball machine, the same spot they convened earlier to plot her fake suicide.

The one who kidnapped her was to cruise through a part of town known for prostitutes and pick one up resembling Alexa. He was to compensate the hooker for oral sex, request she perform it in a parking structure, then catapult her to the ground from the top and leave behind a note.

Alexa urged them not to go through with it, but they didn't listen. Now some poor girl is dead. And Tommy and the police must be distracted by the aftermath. Meaning Dennis and the gangsters may get away with everything. If so, Alexa is soon to end up overseas with her demented ex-boyfriend.

She imagines herself in some remote house in the woods handcuffed to a pipe. Dennis feeding her with a spoon. Trying to convince her this is somehow good for her, that they're still in love, that she's just preventing herself from seeing so.

No. She cannot let that happen. Her odds of escape are much better in the US versus wherever he brings her.

She scans the jumbled items on shelves for a potential weapon. A golf club, a pool cue, an electric guitar.

She is confident she can grab one before the men stop her. But with her hands zip-tied, knocking them all unconscious would be next to impossible.

Her head dips. She thinks. A small, dark object jumps out at her. The black stone of her necklace. Optimism sparks through her. She can use this. But with Dennis watching her in his periphery, must be subtle.

"Den," she says.

The men's voices hush.

"What?" Dennis asks.

"Can I talk to you?"

"I don't want to talk to you right now."

"I know you're mad at me. I was wrong. I've been thinking about how wrong I was. Let me apologize. Please. Come over here and let me apologize."

A moment. He walks to her with slow steps.

On her knees and elbows, she kisses the toe of his shoe, keeping her lips away from the dry blood. "I'm so sorry for what I did. I don't love him. I love you." She peeks up at him.

"Stop it."

She kisses his other shoe. "Stop what? I can't kiss my boyfriend?"

She lowers her chest, touching to the floor the tiny record button on the bottom of the camera necklace charm.

"I would never cheat on you," he says.

"Let's not consider it cheating. After the fire, I felt . . . you were done with me, that we weren't together anymore."

"I could never be done with you. You know that."

"You were right . . . this can be our fresh start." She circles her hands around his calf. And sets her elbow on the top of her charm. She rubs his leg. And presses her elbow down, squeezing the record button. She kisses his thigh. Rises to her feet. Kisses his chest. His lips.

He does not kiss back, but his eyes say he wants to. "Let . . . let me focus," he says. "I'm in the middle of a conversation. A very important conversation. I don't need . . . this. Not now. We'll . . . talk later."

"Okay baby."

He turns, marches toward the gangsters. While his back is to her, she faces a plastic crate with a Shooting Star Pawnshop logo, lines the camera up to it for a few seconds, and presses the necklace button again, stopping the video, sending the clip to her phone. Which might be by Tommy, left behind with him in the Camaro.

She sits back down, hoping he hasn't quit on her.

# FIFTY-THREE

Tommy believes he hears a ding. In the backseat of Chester's squad car. But keeps quiet about it. Could just be in his imagination, another sensory symptom of his untreated head injury. The gigantic hotels outside the windows crowd down on him in the fog, areas of their facades appearing like angry eyes and mouths. He and Chester have already done this pass on Frank Sinatra Drive. No G-Wagons then. None now. No leads over the radio then. None now.

That ding. Tommy notices it again. And decides to test if it's imaginary.

"Hear that?" he asks.

"What?"

"A little noise behind us. A second ago."

"Eh. Sorry, bud."

Tommy turns to the backseat. Scans it for anything electronic. Peeking out from the cardboard box of recovered Camaro belongings is the pink corner of Alexa's phone.

He yanks it out. On the screen a new notification from some app called Cloud Drop that says, *New video uploaded.*

"What're you doing?" Chester asks.

"Someone is trying to contact her. The noise."

"Who?"

Tommy taps the notification. It doesn't open, the screen locked, PIN code required.

Her birthday.

His injured brain tries to recall it. But struggles. A month that is cold. Maybe February. An even-number day.

*0202.* Nope.

*0225.* Nope.

*0210.* Nope.

Maybe January.

*0115.* Nope.

*0110.* Nope.

The phone displays a message:

*After six failed attempts, the device will shut down for security reasons.*

He takes a deep breath.

*0125.*

Yes.

"Ha," he yells.

"What?" Chester asks.

Tommy opens the notification, visits the Cloud Drop app hosting the video. He plays it. The footage is choppy, like the camera were swaying. A leg in jeans. A man's long torso in a tank top, a familiar spiderweb tattoo showing beneath. Dennis.

His voice. Then Alexa's. The camera moves. Soon it

settles. A plastic crate. A logo on it. A name, *Shooting Star Pawnshop.*

"Holy shit," Tommy says.

"Jesus, what?" Chester asks, leaning over, trying to glimpse the screen.

"I was right about the hideout being a cash cleaning business. I just had the wrong one."

"What hideout?"

"I don't think this was a message to Alexa. I think it was a message from her."

"What did she say?"

"Shooting Star Pawnshop. Go."

# FIFTY-FOUR

Cameroon Joe sits in a secondhand La-Z-Boy at the pawnshop, his arm draped over the back cushion, his sunglass-covered gaze aimed at Dennis. He doesn't move for at least a minute. Dennis pretends to ignore him, yet feels uncomfortable in the crosshairs of his stare.

"Nothing from the Hyacinth yet, huh?" Cameroon Joe asks.

Dennis glances at his phone. "Nope."

"Don't you think it's odd we didn't hear from them at all?"

"Maybe they are still conferring."

"Or maybe they already did."

"What do you mean?" Troka asks, lighting a cigarette.

Cameroon Joe says to Dennis, "I find most lawyers

enjoy lawyer jokes. Do you agree?"

Dennis cracks his neck. "Never thought much about it."

"What's interesting is most lawyer jokes are nasty. They tend to be about how lawyers are unscrupulous."

"Big word."

"Thank you. Now imagine jokes about another profession. Let's say garbage men. If you mocked a garbage man for being dirty, do you think he'd enjoy it?"

"What're you getting at?"

"See, I don't think he would. To avoid confrontation, he may chuckle at the joke, pretend it didn't bother him. But it probably would. But lawyers, I think they genuinely like the knocks on them. How do you explain the difference?"

"Beats me."

"I have a theory it's one of two things. First option, deep down lawyers know they're not unscrupulous, so digs about that don't hurt. Sort of like making fun of a skinny person for being fat."

"There you have it. You have cracked the code."

"No. See, I think the second option is the answer." A moment. "You lawyers know the unscrupulous portrayal is true. But unlike the dirty garbage man, you take the portrayal as a compliment."

"Thanks for clarifying. How about we stop—"

"The unscrupulous man gets what he wants at the expense of others. I am a gangster. Some may say I'm unscrupulous myself. But society frowns upon people like me. But not you. And that's where the humor lies. The joke isn't on you, but on the people around you. The people you screw over." Cameroon Joe points at himself and Troka. "People like us."

"Hang on," Troka says. "Are you accusing him of something?"

"The bathroom. Before. I swear he was talking to someone on the phone. How do we know it wasn't the Hyacinth?"

Troka turns to Dennis. "This true?"

A prickle of nerves on the back of Dennis's neck. "Of course not. Who is more trustworthy, me or this street thug?"

"There he goes," Cameroon Joe says. "Proclaiming he's better than someone like me."

"I went to Yale," Dennis says. "I am better than you."

"Your phone's call log. Let's see it."

A pause. "What could I possibly gain by taking a call and telling you I didn't?"

"Oh. I don't know. Ten million dollars."

A laugh of absurdity from Dennis, a trace of nervousness in it. "You're nuts."

"Your phone has access to an off switch. Maybe you told the Hyacinth to send the money to your personal crypto wallet. And you already flipped the switch."

"I'd never do that to you guys. I need you to get me and Alexa out of the country."

"If you had ten million bucks, you could hire plenty of people to get you out of the country."

Troka takes a long drag of his cigarette, his beady eyes scrutinizing Dennis. "Show us your call log."

"You really think I'd betray you?"

"I'd hope not. But only one way to prove it. Show us."

"You can't actually believe this crap? I've had access to your organization's finances since I set up your legal entities. If I was going to rob you, I would've done it then. Why wait till now?"

Cameroon Joe laughs. "I knew it. Look at him.

Still avoiding our simple request." He stands from the La-Z-Boy. "I think I know how we can get him to act." He grips Alexa by the hair, forces her to her feet. Then holds his pistol to her head. "Show us your phone or I show you what her brains look like."

"Stop," Dennis shouts. "She has nothing to do with this."

"Then you should've left her out of it. Not insisted she come here."

Dennis grabs a sharp letter opener off a shelf. "Let her go or I cut your throat."

"Take a step toward me, I pull the trigger."

Troka rubs his brow. "Dennis, show us your phone and make this madness stop."

While Dennis watches Alexa's antsy expression, the pawnshop's security alarm blares.

# FIFTY-FIVE

Smashed glass is scattered at the feet of Tommy and Chester, standing in front of the pawnshop.

"You insane?" Chester asks.

Tommy, who yanked Chester's nightstick off his belt and busted the front window of the closed store, says, "You think we had time for a warrant?" He navigates his hand through the fractured pane, unlocks the door from the inside, and enters. "Come on."

"This is illegal."

"Arrest me if you want. Just do me a favor and wait till I get her out of here first."

Chester huffs, unholsters his gun, and trails him inside with cautious steps. A high-pitched alarm shrieks, sporadic bursts of red light shooting through the shadowy retail space.

Tommy approaches the backdoor, a *STORAGE*

sticker on it. He tightens his grip on the nightstick. The pawnshop is dark for a second. Then reddened with a blast of light. Dark. Red. Dark. Red.

Tommy's free hand grips the doorknob. If any gangster is back there, the alarm must have him spooked, ready to open fire on whatever walks through this door. Tommy should change this.

He recalls Jetmir's voice, then taps into his impersonation skills and says in it, "Hey, it's me. Finally out of the hospital. Sorry about the alarm, set it off by accident."

Tommy barges into the storage room. Among the mess of second-hand items, he sees the gangster who kidnapped Alexa gripping her hair. Behind them Dennis and a man about a foot shorter.

Alexa calls out, "Tommy."

The gangster in sunglasses heaves her onto the floor, then aims his gun at Tommy, who dives behind a metal cabinet.

Chester hustles into the storage room. Tommy notices the gangster moving his pistol toward him and yells, "Get down."

Chester drops his big body the floor.

*Bathunk.* A bullet strikes a shelfed blender right behind where his head just was. He crawls behind a granite pirate statue.

Dennis lifts Alexa off the floor, flips her over his shoulder, and dashes out the rear exit. Tommy lunges forward to chase them, but Chester says, "Don't. You run across the floor, you'd be an easy target. We'll deal with them later."

He's right. Tommy crouches down again, his skin hot with adrenaline.

Chester says into his radio, "Shooting Star Pawnshop. I need backup. Dennis Notch just left. Send search units. Over." He says toward the two men hiding behind columns across the floor, "This joint is going to be flooded with cops any minute. They see you putting up a fight, good chance they're putting you down. Surrender now. Give yourself a chance to live."

The gangster in sunglasses fires at him, missing, taking the nose off the pirate statue. Chester fires back. Hits the column, knocking off a chunk.

Silence for about five seconds.

The short man points a shotgun at Tommy. He pulls the trigger, the screen of a nearby *Mortal Kombat* arcade machine exploding, glass fragments raining onto Tommy's cheek. The man hustles toward the rear exit. Chester shoots him, hitting his lower back. He falls. He is motionless.

Chester's forehead explodes.

A bullet from the other gangster. He topples to the floor, blood pooling around him.

The sight of Chester's corpse turns Tommy's hot skin cold. He eyes his gun. Too far away to grab. The gangster sprints toward the door to the retail area. Tommy whips the nightstick at him. It drills the back of his head. He trips.

Tommy charges at him. The gangster attempts to turn around and shoot him, but Tommy gets to him first. Torpedoes his body into his hip, tackles him into a shelving rack, knickknacks flying off.

The gun goes free. Tommy punches his face, his sunglasses cracking. The gangster grabs a screwdriver fallen from a shelf and stabs Tommy's shoulder. As Tommy grunts, the guy rolls away from him.

He picks up the nightstick and swings it at Tommy's head. Tommy jumps out of the way. He scans the spilt merchandise for a possible weapon. A wooden candlestick.

He grips it, bashes the gangster's ankle with it, then decks his jaw with a left hook. The gangster backhands the nightstick at Tommy's rib, a pulse of pain quaking through his abdomen.

Tommy hammers the candlestick toward his head. Clutching the nightstick with two hands like a baseball bat, the gangster sidesteps the blow and whacks Tommy's weapon, the top half snapping off in a hail of splinters.

The gangster hits Tommy's collarbone, sinking him to a knee. Then lifts the blunt object high for another shot. But before executing it, Tommy stakes him in the gut with the jagged end of the broken candlestick.

The gangster stumbles backward into the wall. His knees give out, his legs at an unnatural angle on the floor beneath him. His one visible eye, behind the broken sunglass frame, angles down at the foreign object in his gut. Blood spills from his mouth. He gurgles. His visible eye closes. He is still.

As Tommy catches his breath, a boom resounds. He falls to the floor. An intense pain in his thigh. His jeans shredded, splattered in blood.

The short gangster isn't dead, lurching toward him with the shotgun and an angry face. Tommy spots the other one's loose pistol. About ten feet away. He crawls toward it, struggling on his hurt leg.

Behind him a *chuh-chuh* of a cocking shotgun.

He looks over his shoulder, notices the barrel staring at him, then looks away, wincing.

A gunshot rings through the storage room. Tommy waits for his head to be ripped apart like Chester's.

But he's still breathing.

He glimpses the gangster. A hole in his throat. He

collapses to the floor.

Tommy pants, his heart slamming, his dazed mind unable to make sense of what happened.

Then he looks toward the doorway into the retail section. A figure in it. Wearing an FBI bulletproof vest.

Jordana.

# FIFTY-SIX

Tommy, still on the storage-room floor, gazes up at Jordana. He blinks a few times, wondering if this image is some delusion from his head injury. But no. This is her.

Her eyes sweep the space, three dead bodies splayed about a disarray of secondhand products. "Clear," she says over her shoulder.

A Black guy in an FBI polo shirt enters, dyed-blond hair. He grimaces at the carnage.

Tommy stands, blood seeping out of the shredded denim over his right thigh. Jordana scopes the wound.

He limps to Chester's corpse, gazes down at what's left of his head. Then punches the pirate statue, even more pain entering his body through his knuckles. "Goddamnit."

Jordana stands next to him. Observes the dead

cop. "Who was he?"

"My friend." Tommy's shot leg gives out. He dips to a knee.

She grabs his shoulders, helps him up. "Let me call you an ambulance."

"No."

"You're torn up with buckshot. And you're bleeding from your . . . God, your ear too? You need medical—"

"Dennis is close. I saw him leave."

A pause. "How close?"

"I didn't hear an engine start. He's on foot. Can't be far. But that could change."

She takes a deep breath. "Stay here, wait for Metro to show. I'm sure they'll have a thousand questions for you. I'll drive around looking for him."

"Fuck that. I'm coming with you."

"You're injured. In no shape to run around after a fugitive. You get into any more action, at best you're going to pass out. At worst, you're going to get yourself killed."

"I'm coming with you." He peers into her eyes without blinking.

"Eh. Fine. Let's go."

She flashes the other agent a thumbs-up. He gives her one back. Tommy follows her into the retail area, the security alarm still flashing and blaring. He grabs a for sale tee shirt off a merchandise rack, ties it around his shot thigh.

She walks outside, climbs into the driver's seat of an unmarked Chevy Traverse, he the passenger's. They pull onto the road.

"Is Dennis with anyone?" she asks.

A moment. "Last I saw, yes."

"Who?"

A moment. "Alexa Thoss."

Jordana's grip tightens on the wheel. She maintains a professional demeanor, yet Tommy can sense her difficulty doing so.

"I heard she committed suicide," Jordana says.

"Some unfortunate lookalike got hurled off a parking structure. Not her. A diversion."

"Umm."

She cruises about five miles below the speed limit through the low-rise business district, glancing out the windows into alleys, Tommy doing the same. No sign of Alexa or Dennis.

"How . . . how did you know I was at the pawnshop?" he asks.

"I didn't."

"What do you mean? Then why'd you show up?"

"I was just following the clues."

"What clues?"

"When I came to your motel room before, I told you I had a theory I wanted to discuss. That was it."

He lifts his eyebrows and slants his head as if to request more detail.

"The townhouse that burnt down," she says. "That Dennis and Alexa were spotted at. I pulled the papers on it. Turns out it was owned by a shell corporation."

"Dennis was the actual owner."

"Figured as much. Probably bought the place to launder his scam profits. Shell corps aren't required to list a human owner, but have to list a company director. Offshore law firms provide this service. Just a name on a document with no actual involvement in the business. The director for the townhouse's corp is an attorney out of Panama. Guy named Enrique Castillo."

"You squeezed him for information?"

"What these offshore directors get paid for is not

giving information, maintaining client secrecy. He's not legally obligated to talk." The sound of sirens. Two cop cars whiz toward the pawnshop. "Once a money launderer forms a relationship with a firm in Panama, they tend to stick with it. Rinse and repeat for all the assets they want to hide from the government. The FBI connected Dennis to the Albanian mob. With his legal background, we figured he was helping them clean their cash."

Tommy nods. "And if Dennis has a relationship with this lawyer in Panama, he probably used the same guy for the Albanians' paperwork."

"Bingo. I cross-referenced a database of businesses operating out of Las Vegas with offshore ownership, and Enrique Castillo as a director. I found a handful, all of them organized crime classics. A tobacco shop. An auto-repair garage. A printshop. Three restaurants. And the Shooting Star Pawnshop. If the Albanians were hiding Dennis Notch in Vegas, my theory was one of these businesses was where."

"I came to a similar conclusion."

"I gave the names to Metro, told them to send a pair of officers to each, ask some questions, look around. The search got derailed at the printshop. They found an Albanian taped up in back, pretty bloody."

"Huh."

"Brought him in for questioning. Wouldn't talk. We figured Dennis was hiding there, got into some altercation with him, then tied him up and split. Then I received a notification the alarm was tripped at the pawnshop. Seemed fishy. So I raced over."

"Ah." He nods a few times. "For a second, I thought you came to save my life."

"I did not. But ... I'm glad it worked out that way."

She gazes into his eyes. A softness in hers reminiscent of how she looked at him before all this calamity in Nevada, when they were a happy couple in California.

She refocuses on the road. "So I guess we're even."

"About what?"

"You saved my life at Dennis's house. And I saved yours at the pawnshop."

"Oh. I guess you're right. Yeah, let's call that even."

Numbness spreads through his right leg. He glances down at it, blood eating through the white tee shirt wrapped around it.

"You feel all right?" she asks.

"Yeah," he lies.

# FIFTY-SEVEN

Dennis, clutching Alexa's arm, paces a sidewalk in the dumpy neighborhood surrounding the pawnshop. The sound of sirens in the distance.

Aware a bound girl slung over his shoulder would provoke a 9-1-1 call from a passing driver, he sliced the zip ties off Alexa's wrists and ankles. He scans the businesses lining Paller Avenue. Plenty dark, closed at this hour. On the nearest lit one, a purple sign for *Lilly's Pleasure Chest*.

He leads Alexa through the door, out of view from the circling cop cars. A wall of sex toys to their left. About a dozen male and female mannequins to their right clad in role-play outfits, nurses, maids, soldiers, dungeon masters.

Perfect. They won't just hide out in here, but pick up disguises.

A female shopper glimpses Dennis's face. He wonders if she recognizes him from the local news. Then she cringes. Relief washes over him, just a reaction to his burns.

Alexa flicks her eyes to the door, as if plotting an escape. Dennis whispers in her ear, "If you run on me, darling, I will pay someone to shoot your brother. And mother. Do you understand?"

A shudder around her chest. "I . . . don't want to go anywhere. I still love you."

"You may have fooled me back at the pawnshop with that act, but I heard how you called out to . . . him . . . when he showed up. Like you wanted him to rescue you from me. That's not fucking love."

He grabs a pink wig, a spiky black one, a leather skirt, and aviator sunglasses. He tucks the items under his arm and leads her toward a sign for *Dressing Rooms*.

The attendant at the counter, a middle-aged bald man with a thin moustache, eyeballs him as he passes.

Dennis pushes open a curtain, steps into a tiny booth with Alexa, hands her the pink wig. "Put it on."

"If you don't think I love you, why're you making me move away with you? Please . . . just leave me behind. Please, Dennis."

"What we had . . . it can . . . come back. We just have to give it time. People can change. We're not predictable. We have the power to surprise ourselves."

She places a tender hand on his cheek. "You just threatened to murder my family. What we had can't come back."

A moment. "Put the fucking wig on, all right?"

She huffs. Sets the wig on her head.

"Your shirt," he says. "Turn it inside out. And lose the necklace." He passes her the skirt. "Then put this on."

She does as he commands. He situates the spiky black wig on his head, stuffing his long hair underneath, and slides on the aviator shades. He gazes at himself and her in the booth's mirror. They look like a regular couple about to attend a Halloween party. A bit outlandish, but in a city like Vegas where outlandish is common, their disguises can work.

He sends a text to his pool guy, Rondo: *Pick us up at Lilly's on Paller.*

Recent immigrant Rondo does not have much money, so Dennis figured he'd take a risk for a payday. He messaged him after the Hyacinth scam fizzled, told him in exchange for safe passage across the state line, he could keep or sell all the left-behind furniture in Dennis's house.

Dennis waits for his reply. Alexa leans against the wall, taps her knuckles against her bottom teeth.

In about fifteen minutes, Rondo texts him: *Here.*

Dennis grabs her hand, ushers her out of the booth, her shorts and necklace left behind. Through the front window, he notices nose ring-wearing Rondo idling in his twenty-year-old Camry.

Dennis veers to the counter, says to the attendant, "We liked them so much, we decided to wear them out."

"You two were back there quite a bit. You okay?"

"Just needed to make sure things fit."

Keying in prices on the register, the attendant stares at Dennis's face. "When you first walked in here, you seemed familiar. Would I know you from anywhere?"

"Sorry sir. Not that I . . . not that I can think of."

The attendant's eyes drift to the right. Dennis follows them. To a cellphone resting on the counter behind an In-N-Out Burger soda cup. An article on it from an ABC-affiliate local news site. The headline, "Ex-Lawyer Wanted for FBI Agent's Kidnap," Dennis's photo beneath.

The attendant's hand creeps under the counter. It inches backward, revealing the end of a crowbar.

Dennis slugs him in the nose. The man hunches forward, blood from his nostrils splattering the white surface.

A shopper screams. Dennis wraps his arm around Alexa's waist, sprints with her toward the door. In the reflection of the window, he sees the attendant chuck the crowbar. Dennis ducks. It soars over him, decapitating a mannequin.

On the other side of the window, Rondo observes with a stunned expression. He pulls the car into gear. The engine growls. He speeds off.

"Wait," Dennis screams, exiting. "Rondo." The Camry doesn't stop. "Fuck."

The ring of cop sirens. Dennis grasps Alexa's arm, hustles a block north. He tugs her onto a side street, a bum in a SpongeBob tee shirt passed out on a bench.

Dennis will need to somehow attain a vehicle and drive out of town, past the police checkpoints, with his wanted face behind the wheel.

A hell of a challenge. But he'll best it. He's smarter than all those cops, all those feds. And that greaseball Dapino.

# FIFTY-EIGHT

Tommy peers out the passenger window of Jordana's Chevy. Barbed wire fencing. Powerlines on old wooden posts. A vagrant pissing on a palm tree. Still no indication of Dennis or Alexa in the roadside shadows.

The alt-rock song on the radio ends. A new one comes on, "Scar Tissue" by the Red Hot Chili Peppers.

For Jordana's twenty-seventh birthday, Tommy bought them tickets to see the band in San Diego. Memories of the night swirl in his head. He guesses hers too.

"Remember that guy?" he asks.

"What guy?"

"At the concert. On acid or whatever. In front of us."

He can tell she tries to fight it, but a grin emerges

on her face. "Yes. I remember that guy."

"What did he say to you again?"

"I forgot."

"No you didn't."

Still grinning, she rolls her eyes. "He said I had nice teeth. Then asked if he could have them in exchange for his popcorn. He made a point to tell me he ordered it with extra butter."

Tommy laughs.

"Then you said something to him," she says, "that he didn't much appreciate."

"No, no he did not."

"I wonder if he thought it through. Like if I told him yes, did he have dental tools waiting in his pocket?"

"And how were you supposed to eat the popcorn without teeth?"

They chuckle.

Silence for a while.

A female voice says from Jordana's radio, "Agent Quick, come in. Over."

Jordana turns off the music, grasps the handset. "Yes. Over."

"Dennis Notch was just spotted at Lilly's Pleasure Chest. Three sixteen Paller Avenue. Over."

"Got it. Over." Jordana plugs the address into the console GPS.

"Floor it," Tommy says.

"Oh Christ," she says, glimpsing his bleeding leg. "That's getting worse." She nods at the console screen. "The address is the opposite direction of the hospital. We go all the way over there and you lose more blood, may not be enough time to get you medical attention." She pulls over.

"What the hell are you doing?"

"I'm letting you out here and calling an ambulance. I'll go to the address alone."

"You're going to need to call an ambulance all right." A moment. "But not for me. For Dennis." He points at the road. "Drive dammit."

She huffs. Then sticks a light on the Chevy's roof and speeds along the GPS route, blazing past a stop sign, a car honking at her.

In about ten minutes, her phone rings, Bluetooth sending the call to the SUV's hands-free system, *Meadows* on the console screen.

She taps a button to answer. "Let me call you back."

"You're going to want to hear this."

"What?"

"We found a laptop. In the pawnshop office."

"Anything good on there?"

"No. In fact, what I found was the opposite of good. It was horrifying."

Jordana takes a deep breath. "I'm on my way to Dennis. I don't have the bandwidth to handle this right now, whatever it is."

"This is more important than Dennis."

"What can be more important than him right now?"

"The bomb he and the Albanians planted at the Hyacinth hotel."

Jordana's mouth hangs open a tad as the Chevy comes to a stop. Glowing purple letters up the road announce *Lilly's Pleasure Chest*. A Metro PD cruiser parked out front, two cops interviewing people on the sidewalk.

Jordana remains inside the idling Chevy, discussing the soon-to-go-off bomb with the other agent. Tommy steps out. Approaches the crowd. Asks it,

"Which way did Dennis go?"

A bald guy with a moustache points north. Tommy jogs that direction.

# FIFTY-NINE

Dennis peeks up at a police helicopter looping the neighborhood. It flies low, the pounding of its blades audible. The spotlight shining from it enters his and Alexa's vicinity. He yanks her into an alley, presses his body and hers against a brick wall.

The glare of the spotlight hits the corner of his sex-shop sunglasses. The beam sweeps through the alley, just missing them.

The sound of the blades softens, the chopper veering south. He continues through the shadows toward his destination, a type of place where he believes he can acquire an automobile.

With a quick Google search on his phone, he found one less than a mile from here. If the police give him any shit on his way out of the city, then state, then country to a non-extradition haven, he'll use the

Hyacinth bomb as a negotiating tool. With the tap of a button on his phone, he has the power to extend the clock, disable it, or detonate.

As his parents often reminded him growing up, he's such a smart boy.

He escorts Alexa east toward Havil Boulevard, the spiky wig wobbling on his head. They move under the lurch of ungroomed palm trees, beside them closed shops, a tarot card reader, a sports memorabilia store, a massage parlor.

*Voo, voo, voo.* A police siren. Sounds just one block over.

A couple dozen feet up is a ratty blue tent, trash scattered in front. Dennis dashes to it, dragging Alexa, the cop siren loudening. He unzips the tent's front.

A fortyish Black man inside with dirt splotches on his cheeks and bare chest, a crack pipe next to him on blankets.

"I'm not going to hurt you," Dennis says, entering the tent with Alexa.

The homeless man's bloodshot eyes enlarge. "Bad demon," he screams. "Bad demon leave alone. Bad."

"We only need to stay in here with you for a minute."

The homeless man skitters into a corner. "Make blood, no. Touch and make blood. No."

Dennis zips up the tent. Through its fabric, the muted shine of police lights. The cop car cruises down the street. The homeless man screams, "Demon. Help. Demon."

Dennis jumps on him, clasps his hand over his mouth. The man writhes, a rancid odor wafting off him.

"Don't hurt him," Alexa says. "He's mentally ill."

"I'm just trying to keep him quiet."

Tears flow from the homeless man's eyes.

"Shh," Dennis says. "Shh."

The police siren distances. He removes his hand from the face of the homeless man, who gasps.

Dennis unzips the tent. Pulls Alexa outside by the wrist. The homeless man scrambles out after them, sucking in air, tears rolling down his cheeks. He looks up at the moon. "No more demon. Please. No more demon."

Gripping Alexa, Dennis continues toward his destination.

# SIXTY

Tommy jogs along Paller Avenue as fast as his shotgun-blasted leg lets him, scanning the shadows for Dennis and Alexa. He peeks down a side street. Nothing but a couple parked cars and straggly palm trees.

He trots to the next side street, blood dripping from his thigh, dotting the pavement under him. An awning for a closed sports memorabilia store. Movement nearby. A man. Black. Shirtless. He walks in a circle, pulling at his hair.

"Hey," Tommy says to him.

The man's bloodshot eyes fixate on him.

"Did you notice a tall man with a blond girl around here?"

"Beware the demon." He seems out of his mind, yet with sincerity in his voice.

"You saw a demon?"

"Demon with girl. Hair not yellow. Pink." The man chews on the heel of his hand.

"What did this demon look like?"

"Black eyes. Face melted."

Tommy thinks for a moment. Though he saw Dennis at the pawnshop for only a few seconds, he noticed burns on his face, must be from the townhouse fire. Maybe that's what "face melted" means.

"Which way did the demon go?" Tommy asks.

A twitchy nod from the man, east toward a busier street. "No you go. Don't go to demon."

"I'll take my chances. Thank you."

The man looks away, returns to pulling at his hair, walking in a circle.

Tommy jogs to the end of the block, his hurt leg hitching. He arrives on a double yellow line road, *Havil Boulevard* on its sign.

He peers left, a strip mall, all its windows dark. No Dennis. He peers right, more closed businesses. But in the distance, about a mile away, he notices a lit red-and-yellow image on a pole, the fog obscuring it. The logo for Cluck-Cluck Fried Chicken, a popular West Coast chain.

They're open late. And have drive-through windows. The easiest type of car to steal is one already running.

The fog doesn't permit him detailed visibility, but Tommy guesses Dennis is up ahead, moving toward the restaurant. Excitement and nerves course through him.

If Dennis is indeed on his way there, he has a head start. No way Tommy can catch up to him with this bad leg.

He reaches into his pocket, pulls out a hundred-dollar bill. A pair of headlights travels along Havil. A Saturn. Tommy steps into the road waving his arms, cutting it off. An alarmed, mid-twenties female behind the windshield. She halts.

Tommy juts his arm forward, making sure she can see the hundred. "I want to give this to you," he says. "I hurt my leg. And I need to get up the road. A hundred bucks for a lift."

Her gaze on the money. Then his bloody leg. "No. Now get out of my way."

"Couple minutes max. You have nothing to lose."

"I don't want blood all over my seat."

"I won't even get in. I'll stay out here. The roof. Slip the cash through the window."

She mumbles something to herself. Then rolls down the passenger window about an inch. He deposits the bill, then crawls up to the roof, clutches the sides of the car. "Okay, go."

.

# SIXTY-ONE

The Saturn drives about thirty miles per hour along Havil Boulevard, wind whipping into Tommy's face, his knuckles aching from hanging on.

He peers at the sidewalk bordering the road. In about a minute and a half a figure materializes in the fog, about ten feet from the Cluck-Cluck Fried Chicken lot. A tall man. Spiky, artificial-looking hair. In his grip the forearm of a girl in a pink wig.

Dennis and Alexa.

Tommy slaps the passenger window of the Saturn. "Stop."

The driver whales the brakes. The force hurls Tommy off the roof. His right side bashes into the pavement. Pain through his hip, rib, and shoulder.

"Tommy," Alexa says, above the screech of the Saturn wheels speeding off.

Dennis stops trotting. He removes his sunglasses, revealing his burns. Takes in the sight of Tommy on the ground. Then gallops toward him.

Tommy rises to his knees. Dennis kicks his upper back, slamming him down to the pavement. Then climbs on top of him, throws a punch at his head. Tommy leans to the side, Dennis's knuckles grinding against the asphalt.

He grunts. Tommy turns over, curls his good leg up to his chest, and kicks Dennis off him. While Dennis backpedals, Tommy stands. Then says to Alexa, "Run inside, have someone call nine-one-one."

Her pink head nods. She turns around. Dashes into the lot. Dennis chases her. Tommy goes after him, not as fast with his shot leg.

Dennis grasps Alexa's shoulder. A couple seconds later, Tommy latches onto the back of Dennis's tank top. Dennis spins, something metallic gleaming in the shine of the overhead Cluck-Cluck sign.

By the time Tommy can tell what it is, it is penetrating him. A letter opener pierces his flesh a few inches up from his hip. Two squiggles of blood rush out from the tear in his shirt, form a figure eight on the brass.

Dennis attempts to drive the blade in farther, to shred a vital organ. Tommy clenches his wrist. The men's arms remain in a forceful deadlock for a few seconds, the blade remaining in place.

But Tommy's loss of blood must've sapped his energy, his resistance fading, the blade eking deeper into his body. Cries of panic from customers on the drive-through line.

Dennis gnashes his teeth, the tension in his expression opening some burn wounds, dabs of blood surfacing on his face.

A flurry of napkins. Dennis falls to a knee. Behind him is Alexa, in her hands a metal napkin holder from one of the restaurant's outdoor tables. His wig at his side. She must've just clobbered his head. She takes a deep breath, then sprints toward the entrance.

Tommy yanks the blade out of his flesh, pain radiating from the cut all the way up to his throat.

He swipes the blade at Dennis's face. He ducks, punches Tommy in his new wound. The waves of pain thicken. He punches him again. And again, Tommy dropping the letter opener.

Dennis reaches for it. But Tommy clasps his hair, forces his head back. Then elbows the bridge of his nose. A spurt of blood from his nostrils.

Tommy shoves him into an outdoor table. Then turns, runs toward the knife. But faster Dennis catches up to him, circles his arms around him, and steps toward the blade.

With a longer reach than Tommy, he'd be sure to pluck it from the ground once close. Tommy needs to move this fight in another direction. He grips Dennis's jeans, lunges away from the knife toward the restaurant.

Dennis labors to direct them the other way. But Tommy resists. Leveraging the power in his good leg, he lunges again toward the restaurant, carrying Dennis with him. And again. And again. They're no more than three feet from the front window.

The sound of police sirens enters the atmosphere.

Tommy crouches, torquing his body. Then springs upward, launching himself and Dennis at the window. Dennis hits it first, bashing the glass. A broken edge slices Tommy's arm just above his elbow, but Dennis lands first, the dozens of slivers on the floor digging into his back.

Screams from the customers huddled inside, Alexa among them.

Dennis grimaces, blood running from his back onto the hodgepodge of cracked glass on the brown tile floor. Tommy rips the pawnshop tee shirt off his leg, wraps it around his hand, and picks up the largest shard in sight, about six inches. Dennis lifts his lacerated torso from the floor. He throws a right hook at Tommy. Who dodges it, and jams the shard into his heart.

A choking noise from Dennis. He peers down at his impaled chest. More choking noises. He finds Alexa's face among the onlookers. He takes a deep breath. And says, "I'll always love you."

His torso drops back to the floor, the glass stake protruding from it.

# SIXTY-TWO

Tommy plops into a seat inside Cluck-Cluck, agonizing pain biting through his body. He rips a wad of napkins from the holder on the table and presses it against his letter-opener wound. Within seconds, all the white of the napkins is red.

While police sirens wail, Alexa hovers over Dennis's dead body, the pink of her wig framing her flawless complexion. She doesn't blink.

Through the broken window, Tommy notices six guns-drawn Metro PD officers storming through the crowd of employees and customers in the parking lot.

Their steps slow when they make out the face of the glass-staked corpse. The cop leading the way, a mid-forties guy with thick, hairy arms, enters the restaurant through the spike-edged window opening. He glimpses Alexa and Tommy, the only two inside besides Dennis.

Eyeing Tommy's bruised, bloodied body, the cop says into his shoulder radio, "We're going to need an ambulance."

Jordana and the Black agent with the dyed hair rush inside. Her eyes widen.

"Oh no," the male agent says.

Jordana takes a deep breath. "Okay, stay calm. Let's just . . . stay calm."

"He's dead," Tommy says. "It's over."

"What about the bomb?"

That's right. So much going on. He almost forgot. A fucking bomb.

Jordana kneels on a bed of stained-red glass at Dennis's side, checks his pockets, pulls a cellphone from one. She taps on the screen. Screams, "Shit."

"Locked?" the male agent asks.

"With no thumbprint option. We need the four-digit passcode. Can you hack into it?"

He checks his watch. "Not in nine minutes."

"What's going on?" Alexa asks.

Jordana glares at her. "You . . . please . . . stay out of this. This is an FBI matter." She points at the parking lot. "And a closed scene. Wait outside."

Alexa doesn't budge.

Tommy climbs off his seat toward the others. His aching body falters. He trips, catches himself on a garbage receptacle. He looks at Alexa. "You dated him. Must've seen him type in his PIN, right?"

She folds her arms, an anxious hitch of her shoulders. "I don't know. I never paid attention." A moment. "A bomb is really about to go off?"

"Yes," the male agent says.

"His birthday," Tommy says. "What's his birthday?"

"Uh. November. November sixteenth."

"Three ones and a six," he says to Jordana.

She taps Dennis's phone four times. Shakes her head.

"He have a lucky number he played at the casino?" Tommy asks Alexa.

"He didn't . . . he didn't gamble."

Tommy places his hands on Alexa's upper arms. They tremble. "What was important to him that could be associated with a number? A hobby?"

"He didn't really have any hobbies. He did his business stuff. When he was done for the day, he'd hang out with me."

"That's it."

"What's it?"

"You."

"Me?"

"Yes." A moment. "Before he died, the way he looked at you. What he said. He really loved you."

"I . . . yeah, I know. So?"

"So he's been using that phone on the run. It's new. Meaning he set the passcode up after he met you. It could involve you."

"Just seven minutes left," the male agent says.

"How would it involve me?" Alexa asks. "He never mentioned any special number to me or anything."

An image streaks across Tommy's hurt brain. It's trying to tell him something. A grainy image. Surveillance footage. From Rose Lounge. The day Dennis met Alexa.

"Zero two, twenty-three," Tommy shouts at Jordana.

She taps Dennis's screen four times. She kicks her head back in surprise. "I'm in." She scurries to the male agent, hands him the phone. He works the screen with fast thumbs. Thirty seconds pass. A minute.

The numbness in Tommy's leg stretches through the rest of his body. His head goes light. He sits on the floor, a couple feet from Dennis, rests his back on the base of the counter.

Jordana and Alexa huddle behind the male agent, peering at the screen over his shoulders. He taps and swipes for about another minute.

Then lets out a long breath.

He grins. "Disabled."

Jordana claps. Alexa bends forward in relief, hands on her knees. The pink wig falls off her head.

All three gaze at Tommy. "How did you guess zero two, twenty-three?" Jordana asks.

He nods at Alexa. "February twenty-third. Their anniversary."

The remaining energy in Tommy's body slips away. He passes out.

# SIXTY-THREE

Tommy listens to the soft hum of the machinery in his hospital room, a view of the Strip in the distance outside his third-floor window, the neon signs bare in the daylight.

A nurse enters with a smile and plastic cup of orange juice. "How you holding up?" she asks.

"Like I fell off the Empire State Building."

"According to the doctor, you're lucky you didn't end up brain damaged or dead."

"Sometimes I think I might already be brain damaged to do some of the things I do."

She hands him the orange juice. "Well, this won't cure brain damage. But the vitamin C should help with some other things."

He takes the cup, sips from a straw while she checks the readings on the machines he's hooked up to.

A knock on the door. They look to it. Jordana in the entryway.

The nurse, who must sense Jordana intends to speak in private, says, "I'll uh . . . give you two the room, come back later to check in." She leaves.

Jordana smiles at her, then enters, closes the door. Hands behind her back, head down, she moseys toward Tommy, sits in a bedside chair. "Remember the last time I visited you in a room like this?" she asks.

The first time they kissed, in a hospital in Imperial County, California after taking down the men behind his sister's murder.

"Of course," he says.

She says nothing for a while. "I'm sorry about yesterday. How I acted at the motel. That . . . wasn't me."

"Crazy day."

"If you happen to speak to Alexa, tell her I'm sorry too." A pause. "I won't be pursuing blackmail charges against her. I'll be recommending the FBI pin the crime on Dennis, say he coerced her to participate. Even if that isn't . . . entirely true."

"That's . . . good of you."

"Yeah . . . well." She rubs her forehead. "Here's the thing. You're right. Yesterday was a crazy day. We both probably said things . . . and did things . . . we shouldn't have. And I know I told you it was over. But . . . do we really want to throw away something great just because of one crazy day?"

To his shock, she is giving him another chance. An image flashes in his mind of him in her family's next Christmas photo.

But then he sees another image, Dennis at the fried chicken restaurant, the glass stake jutting from his chest, his lungs mustering up the air for his final words, telling Alexa he'll always love her.

Jordana deserves the same level of unconditional commitment from a man. Though she apologized for snapping at Alexa at the motel, doubts remain in his mind about proposing to her after seeing that side of her. He wishes he could give her what she deserves. But isn't certain he could.

"What we've had was great," he says. "And it'll always be great. Even if . . . we don't spend the rest of our lives together." A moment. "Maybe we can give it another try someday. But I don't want to waste your time unless I'm sure."

She is quiet for a few seconds. Then nods. A tear rolls down her cheek. "That's just like you."

"What is?"

A moment. "You're protecting me." She kisses his forehead. "Bye Tommy."

He watches her walk to the door. Then disappear on the other side.

# SIXTY-FOUR

"T, I'm thinking I keep at the machines here for a little, then maybe we throw down some light fare at one of the many eateries off the casino, back to the suites for a power nap, then we all shower up and leave ourselves a solid forty-five cushion to get to the ventriloquist show," Josh says, sitting on a slot stool at the Hyacinth casino. "What's your temp on that agenda?"

Tommy stands behind him sipping a Bud Light. For helping avert the bomb threat, he was comped a couple suites here. On Josh's lap is Michelle, the girl he's been seeing in San Diego, twenty-nine, curly brown hair, cute.

"This is your thank-you trip for busting me out of jail," Tommy says. "You make the agenda. I go with it."

Josh grins. "I can't wait for this performance

tonight. How do they do it, not moving their mouth when they talk? Are the words somehow coming out the nostrils? It's all connected back there, the piping. The nose, T. Got to be. That's what I got my money on."

"Oh, the nose must be pivotal," Michelle says.

"Right babe?" Josh says.

"It's been too long since I've enjoyed live ventriloquism. Can't wait either."

"What's your tally, live performances?"

"Three. One was my sister's friend, in the common area of her dorm. So maybe I shouldn't count that. So two."

"Two more than me. I've seen clips on YouTube, but the real McCoy . . . in person . . . come on."

"Buckle up."

"Speaking of your sister, you sure she doesn't want a few bucks?"

"Gives her something to do. Don't sweat it."

Josh turns to Tommy. "T, Michelle's sister is a lifesaver. Agreed to feed the lobsters while I'm out here."

Michelle looks around. "This casino is very nice. Don't get me wrong. Tommy, again, appreciate you so much for offering Josh and me a room. But we were talking before and . . . don't you think a touch of marine life could add some ambience?"

Josh says, "Tell me one establishment that wouldn't benefit from a fish tank. Now tell me one fish tank with the appeal of a lobster one. Sharks don't count. I'm talking practical."

"You're a visionary," Michelle says.

Josh kisses her.

Tommy smiles at them. He receives a text message on his phone from Alexa: *Walking up.*

In a couple minutes, she appears in the casino, men checking her out. Tommy waves at her.

"That the girl you're saying goodbye to?" Josh asks.

"I won't be long."

In the past, Josh would've gawked at Alexa. But his attention is already back on Michelle.

Still with a slight limp from the shotgun blast a few days back, Tommy walks to his visitor. "No more Nevada, huh?" he asks.

"First time in my life."

"Where to?"

"South Carolina. With my brother. He's all healed up, just like you. We both decided it was time for a change."

"Wow. Kurt too. Tell him I say hi."

"We're going to try to be roommates. I have some money saved up from . . . from you know . . . what I used to do. Enough to get us both on our feet. He's going to look for a job in construction. Think I'll check out some college classes."

"That sounds great."

"Someone once told me I had more to offer than I thought. Guess I'm taking a chance on his advice."

He chuckles. "All I ask is one favor?"

"Uh oh. What?"

"Make sure you pick a town with a CVS."

She giggles. And holds out her arms. They hug. "I'm happy I met you, Tommy."

"I'm happy I met you too."

As compatible as they might be, they are at different places in their lives. He never considered turning what they had serious, and doubts she did either. He may never see her again. Or the future could have something else in store for them. He will only know in time.

"Wishing you the best," she says. "In . . . whatever is next."

"Not sure what's next."

"Well, I'm sure you'll figure something out."

A grin on his face, he waves.

She does too. Then turns, walks the way she came, slot machines ringing around her. Soon she vanishes among the crowd.

# SIXTY-FIVE

Tommy, in shorts and flip-flops, sorts through his mail at his surf shack in San Diego. All junk besides an envelope from Helga Wichita, the Special Agent in Charge of the local FBI branch. He rips it open. Pulls out that Ziploc bag with his hair in it, a handwritten note accompanying. He reads:

*Glad I didn't have to use this. Also glad you got back from Vegas alive.*

*-Wichita*

Tommy, smiling, gazes at it for a couple seconds, then tosses it and the hair in the garbage. His gaze catches the fake Patek Philippe watch from Grandpa Dapino on the counter. He'd been thinking a lot about it. Debated wearing it again. Didn't feel right. Considered throwing it out. Also didn't feel right. He decided he'll do neither, just hold onto it.

He takes a deep breath, looks around the house. It feels empty with Jordana's photos off the wall. But he doesn't regret his choice.

He heads outside, his limp almost gone. Gets in his Ford Explorer and drives to a place in La Jolla he's passed before. He pulls into its parking lot, walks through the front door.

A middle-aged woman in a blue vest with the place's logo on it says, "Welcome to the La Jolla Animal Center." A few feet behind her is a door. Barking on the other side. "What brings you in?"

"Your website says you do adoptions?"

She smiles. "Follow me." She opens the door, revealing dogs of many colors, shapes, and sizes. "What kind are you looking to adopt?"

"You know anything about them? Where they came from, that sort of thing?"

She points at a Boston Terrier. "This one's owner became a bit too old to care for her on his own. So called us to find her a new home." She stops at another cage, provides some background on the dog inside, then the one above it.

Then she strides to a puppy, part-Husky, part-something else. Its warm eyes hang on Tommy. "This mix was recovered from a local hardware store running dog fighting afterhours," she says. "He was too young to fight. But they bred him to get in the ring soon. Thankfully the San Diego PD found out about the operation and broke it up before that."

"I'm glad the San Diego PD finally did something right."

An absent giggle from her. "What . . . eh, what exactly do you mean, sir?"

"Don't worry about it." Tommy smiles at the dog. Then turns to the clerk. "I've got a good feeling about this guy."

"So exciting." She opens the cage, the dog running to Tommy.

"Hey," Tommy says. "How you doing, pal?"

"You seem like you'll be a great dog dad." A moment. "Will you be caring for him yourself . . . or is there a dog mom at home too?"

"No dog mom. Maybe one day. But I'm in . . . no rush."

"Better not to rush that. Got a name in mind for your new friend?"

Tommy looks at the dog's face. "Yeah. I just got back from Vegas. I'm thinking Sinatra."

"Seems like good luck."

Tommy pets Sinatra. "I have a feeling we'll be all right even without any luck."

# ABOUT THE AUTHOR

*EDGE OF CHAOS* is book 2 in Ted Galdi's Tommy Dapino series. Ted is an Amazon #1 bestselling thriller author, featured by *Kirkus* magazine, ABC, FOX, iHeartRadio, and many other media outlets.

For a free book, visit his website at tedgaldi.com.

www.ingramcontent.com/pod-product-compliance
Lightning Source LLC
Chambersburg PA
CBHW072129250626

47159CB00007B/2624